COCKY KILT

JOLIE VINES

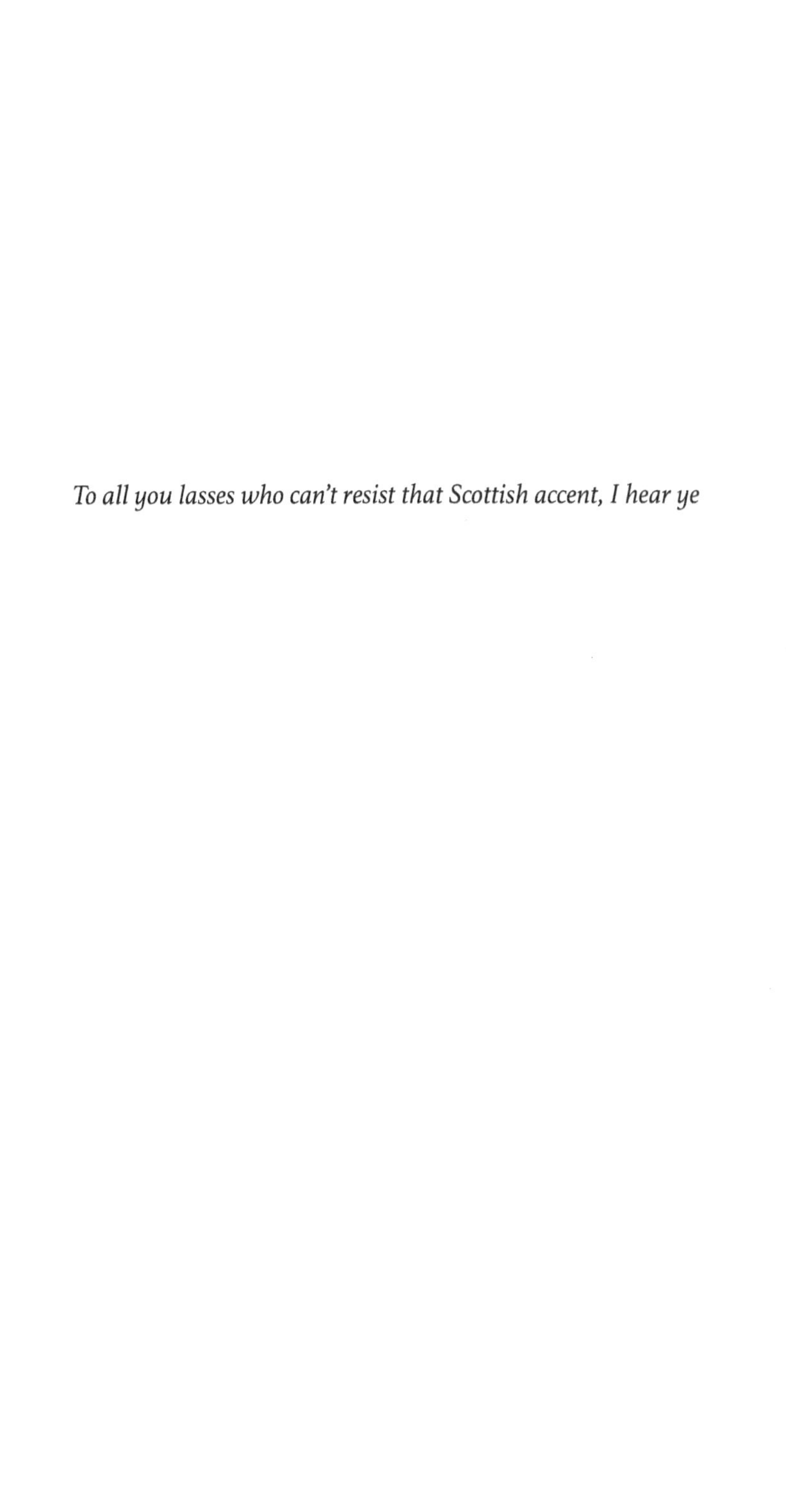

To all you lasses who can't resist that Scottish accent, I hear ye

READER NOTE

Dear reader,

The steamy book you've just picked up is one I've written in the Cocky Hero world, based on stories by Penelope Ward and Vi Keeland.

It also links to my *Wild Scots* series, with Ewan popping up in one of the books. If you swoon for the sexiest accent in the world – Scottish – I've got you covered. Jump back and start with *Hard Nox (Wild Scots, #1)*.

Read them all? Go meet their daddies. The *Marry the Scot* series features the first generation of McRaes and Fitzroys.

Best of all? I'm not done. There's more to come in the new *Wild Mountain Scots* series.

Jolie x

BLURB

I thought the scenery would be the highlight of my working trip to Scotland, then a dark-haired, kilted Highlander walks into the bar.

That swoony Scottish accent.

Dark eyes and a sexy smirk.

Would anyone blame me for a quick holiday romance? Except if I want to keep my job, Ewan is off limits. I need to lock down my lust.

For a former poor kid who's used to deprivation, this should be easier.

But my cocky Scot doesn't agree, and he's hell bent on changing my mind.

--

Cocky Kilt is a cute and steamy romp between a New York lass and a determined Scot. Expect sexting after dark and a love-conquers-all happy ending.

Written in the Cocky Hero Club world, Hailey, our heroine, is first featured in Park Avenue Player by Vi Keeland and Penelope Ward.

A COURAGEOUS, MODERN WOMAN

ailey - Autumn

Rain splattered the windows, and the plane swung wide over the Scottish airstrip, the fall weather welcoming me in style. Four days ago, I'd left New York City in balmy sunshine. My last few days traveling between gorgeous tourist locations in the UK had been exciting and mostly dry.

Scotland had prepared a torrential downpour for my arrival.

For my first official business trip in my new job, the universe was sure throwing the book at me.

Another gust of wind swiped at the plane, but we touched down with just a bump. Passengers applauded, and I let out a sigh of relief.

Finally, I was here: the last location I had to scout before returning home. I was more than ready to witness the splendors of Scotland I'd heard so much about. Even exhaustion and a storm couldn't dent the thrill.

On the flight, I'd read a romance book in which the hero

was a Scotsman. A stern, *huge* man. After my last embarrassing disaster of a flirtation, I'd needed the distraction. If any handsome Highlander wanted to fall madly in love with me over the weekend, I wouldn't mind.

Collecting my checkerboard Louis Vuitton carry-on bag, I extracted my suit jacket and shook out the wrinkles. The poor-kid version of me had never gotten used to having money, so I shot the thin jacket a disgruntled glare for daring to be untidy and joined the queue to clatter down the metal steps, ready to make a run for the airport. At the plane's exit, I peered out.

The downpour thundered. I took a deep breath, held my bag over my head, and bolted.

Rain drenched me, slapping my skin, no letup as I sprinted over the blacktop. Inside the tiny terminal building, I wiped the water from my eyes and shivered through arrivals.

At the taxi rank, I threw myself into the warm car with barely disguised relief.

"Where can I take ye?" the driver asked, his accent so thick I barely understood him

"The inn at Cock Bridge," I replied.

Wow. Managed that without laughing.

My driver gave me a nod, and we were on our way.

For a while, I watched the pretty scenery go by, but this past week had done a number on me, and my eyelids drooped.

Despite my soaking, I couldn't regret anything about this trip. I was only here because my boss, Diane, contracted stomach flu at the last minute and had no one else she could send.

With my minor Scotland obsession, I was looking

forward to this place more than any other on the working vacation.

Still, I felt my mind shutting down, lulled by the rhythmic movement of the windshield wipers and the rush of the tires on the road.

Sometime later, I jerked awake, groggy and disorientated. "Where are we?" I mumbled and checked my phone.

"Nearly there. You're American," my driver observed, grinning. "Ye here to see the battlefields? Or maybe where *Outlander* was filmed? We get a lot of Americans come in on the tours and the cruise ships."

"I'm here on business but I'd like to see as much as I can." I slid a glance at the man. "Bet you get sick of all the foreigners, right?"

"Naw, lass. It's our bread and butter." He pulled up outside a cute stone building, warm lights glowing through the windows. "Well, most of us welcome tourists. The man who owns this place is a right miserly bugger. Steer clear of Old Mac, aye?"

That didn't bode well. I paid the bill and climbed from the car on shaky legs, taking a full and deep breath. Drizzle floated in the air, gentler now than the torrent at my arrival. Tomorrow, I'd get to tour this land—a pretty spot at the foot of a mountain in the Cairngorms National Park—but right now, I needed a meal and a glass of wine.

Then sleep. Lots of it.

My friendly driver handed over my bag, and I entered the front door of the inn, ducking under the low frame. Inside, a warm and cozy space spread out. At one end, a log fire blazed in a hearth, a fluffy black-and-white dog reclining on the flagstone floor in front of it, and customers perched at the bar, pints of amber beer in hand. To my right, more people sat at clusters of tables and chairs, and I glimpsed a more formal dining area at the far end.

The rich scent of cooking and the babble of cheerful conversations welcomed me.

A pretty picture of rural bliss.

With my phone, I quickly took a couple of shots. Diane would love this place. I could easily picture it being the perfect base for our exclusive clients to explore the Highlands.

A young woman clipped over, drying her hands on her apron. She beamed. "Hello! Are ye here for a room?"

"Please! It's booked under Diane Kudrow, but she had to cancel. I'm Hailey."

"Welcome! We're glad to have ye. Follow me and we'll get ye set."

The woman gave me a guest book to sign then showed me upstairs to a neat room before leaving me to settle in. The soft-looking bed beckoned, but I knew if I laid my head on it, like in the cab, I'd be asleep in minutes. Instead, I freshened up in the bright little bathroom, brushed my long blonde hair out of its ponytail, my earlier soaking giving me damp, frizzy curls, then changed into jeans and a shirt.

A peek outside my window showed me the dark afternoon had turned into evening, and the snug bar was calling my name. At the top of the stairs, I hesitated, testing my emotions. When I'd informed my Uncle Hollis about the trip, he'd frowned and told me how he'd worry about me being alone in a strange place. But I wasn't nervous. Not at all. People fascinated me.

New places had me itching to explore.

I dropped down the stairs, my smile at the ready.

*A*n hour later, and a light meal plus two glasses of wine inside me, I chuckled along to the story a woman was telling. The Cock Bridge Inn was full of my fellow countrywomen, here to do exactly what the cab driver had said—see the sites from the *Outlander* TV show, and maybe find their own handsome Scot.

I'd homed in on a friendly group and taken up their invite to sit with them. This was the perfect way to find out what visitors here really wanted and whether the inn was as good as my first impression.

The door swung wide, drawing my attention.

And that of every female in the room.

A man stomped in, shaking rain from his dark hair as he closed out the evening. He grinned and raised a hand in answer to a greeting from the bartender.

My gaze drifted over his body. From his handsome face with a wide smile, down to his heavy combat boots, and lingering over his kilt.

A real life kilt!

God, was that sexy.

"Oh my," Mirabelle said, the octogenarian to my right, lowering to peek over her glasses. "I like this place more and more."

"How's it hanging, Ewan?" The woman who'd shown me to my room breezed past, collecting glasses.

Ewan, as he must be, hung his dripping jacket near the fire and raised an eyebrow. "Eh. A tad chilled and shrunken, but that's the weather."

"Gross!" she trilled back, raising laughter in the room.

The newcomer joined the old boys nursing their drinks at the bar, and leaned in to chat to the bartender. Conversation resumed around me, and I tried to pull my focus away.

Yet when I next glanced over, the cocky Scot was gazing right back at me.

My body zinged at the eye contact.

A month ago, I'd made a fool of myself over a guy. At a party my company had thrown, I'd been thrilled with the freedom of my first job and let myself be chatted up by Andrew, a sales rep from another branch.

In a dark corner, he'd made a move on me.

At college, I'd had a couple of serious boyfriends but I'd never played the field. But I was twenty-three now and had no intention of missing out on the fun everyone else seemed to be having. Emboldened, I'd welcomed Andrew's advances.

Until Josie from Accounts took me to one side and whispered how Andrew was a notorious womaniser.

And married.

Ugh. Such a jerk. So embarrassing to have been caught in his trap when all I wanted to do was make a good impression in my career. At least I'd had this opportunity to escape for a few days. After I returned to New York, I'd start over and hope everyone else had forgotten.

I zoned back into the conversation at the table and stole another glance at the handsome man at the bar. My pride might've been dented, but my libido wasn't. I'd made a mistake but I still had a point to prove to myself.

I was a courageous, modern woman who could get hers and walk away contented. What better than to do that on a working vacation? Maybe finding out whether the Scot at the bar really did have anything on under his kilt.

Oof. The alcohol was going to my head a little too much.

"You're going to love Scotland. It has so much to offer. History, culture, and the men!" Mirabelle gave me a poke with her elbow. "More wine, dear?"

I eyed the kilted man once more to see him, again, staring right back at me.

"Yes, please." I held up my glass. "To all that. I don't mind if I do."

2

PURE ANIMAL ATTRACTION

*E*wan

Briana bumped my shoulder with hers, my annoying brat of a younger cousin. "What did he do today?"

"How do ye know I've a problem with Da?"

She rounded the bar to the other side and stacked her collected glasses into the dishwasher, steam sticking her hair to her forehead. "You're on the whisky. Ye never drink unless Old Mac is causing problems."

"True." I took a deep sip, draining my tumbler and enjoying the burn down my throat. "Today, he decided to close the road leading to Falmer's Cairn. Claiming some nonsense about coaches causing damage to the standing stones. I only found out after an irate tour owner called and gave me an earful."

Briana tutted in sympathy and busied on with her work.

Old Mac, my father, was becoming a hazard. He'd always been eccentric, but now, he was actively disrupting the McClintock family business. Over a dozen adults worked for us, all locals, and their families relied on the income tourism brought. We were right at the end of the season now, and if Da caused any more mayhem, next year would see the tours going elsewhere.

It was a real problem, and one I wasn't sure how to fix.

As it had multiple times already this evening, my attention found its way to the gorgeous lass sitting with the old dears across the room. With waves of yellow hair and a pretty smile on her pink lips, she was a vision on a gloomy day.

Then, like before, she peeked over at me.

My blood warmed, and I raised an eyebrow, enjoying the flush on her cheeks as she glanced away.

I'd been single for the best part of a year now, with my childhood sweetheart up and leaving me to move to the city. It had been a rough break-up, but I understood her reasons for going. Just like she knew I couldn't follow her. She'd been back to see her folks once or twice, and we'd met as friends.

Well, as friendly as I could be with someone who'd taken my heart and drop-kicked it.

I hadn't tried a relationship since, unable to imagine trusting someone again. Occasionally, I'd considered scratching an itch with the tourists who saw me as a novelty. I wore my kilt with pride and didn't mind if the lasses enjoyed the view. To date, though, I hadn't taken anyone up on their offer.

"Another?" Pat, who was serving tonight, asked.

I handed over my glass. "Just one. I have a meeting first thing tomorrow, if Da doesn't blow it." Then a thought occurred to me. Aside from the lass checking me out, everyone else here was middle aged or above. On the phone, the person I was meeting had sounded younger. "Diane Kudrow hasn't checked in yet, has she?"

Diane ran a boutique travel agency in the US, and I was

desperate to get onto one of her tours. We'd host their clients in the inn, take them around the local ruins, all over the Highlands, and for a very nice fee that would keep us on our feet for years.

But I'd checked the guest book, and the woman hadn't signed in. Perhaps her flight was late.

Patrick poured me another whisky. My second, and last, double of the evening. "Naw. Not a name I've heard."

Briana returned with more glasses.

Patrick raised his chin at her. "Not seen a Diane yet, have ye?"

"No, but the pretty blonde Ewan's eyeing up is named Hailey." She gave me a wink.

"Hailey, aye?" I murmured. Bonnie name for a very attractive woman. "Perhaps I should go over and help the group with some local knowledge."

As if she heard, the lass stood and made her way over.

Briana snorted, and I stood taller.

With a shy look at me, the woman leaned in to Patrick. "Hey, sorry to bother you. One of the ladies I'm with is turning eighty tomorrow. They're staying here another night, but I'll be gone by then. Can I buy a bottle of champagne now and you surprise her with it tomorrow?"

Patrick raised his eyebrows. "Absolutely." He grabbed an order book and took payment.

"Kind of ye," I said, low.

The lass turned, her cheeks pinker still. "They've been lovely to me. Stranger in a strange land and all."

"What part of the States are ye from?"

She didn't answer for a second, just gazing at me. "Uh, what? Sorry. Um, NYC, though I spent a lot of my teenage years in Connecticut with my family. I'm guessing you're a local?"

I put out a hand. "You guess right. I'm Ewan."

"Hailey." She took my fingers in a brief press.

My heart thudded, some kind of chemical reaction sparking on my skin.

"Whoa," Hailey muttered.

She felt it, too. *Christ.*

The urge came over me to press my advantage. A little flirting never hurt anyone, and already, from her proximity alone, I felt fifty times better. "Can I get ye a drink?"

Hailey pursed her pink lips. "Is that a pick-up line?"

I choked on a laugh. "Maybe."

"Are you single?"

"What kind of question is that? Aye, I am."

She folded her arms. "Lift up your hand."

Holding back a laugh, I did, and she scrutinised my ring finger, looking for a dent or a tan line, I imagined.

"Hey, Briana," I hollered to my cousin. "How single am I?"

Everyone knew how I'd been dumped.

Briana rolled her eyes. "Tragically so. My cousin is a poor wee thing."

Hailey giggled. "I believe you. And I have a better idea. Why don't you join my group? Several of the ladies have expressed fascination with your...kilt. I'm sure they'd love to ask you questions about what it's like to live here."

An hour and another couple of drinks down the hatch, and I was merry. The ladies were a hoot and Hailey captivating. She didn't seem the type to be on an all-female cruise and coach tour, like her friends were. That tended to be for ladies who'd become widowed, or wealthy singletons who wanted to see the world and make like-minded new friends.

Where the older women were more than happy to share their life stories with me, Hailey kept her cards close to her chest. Apart from her name and where she was raised, I had nothing on her.

Her small, infuriating grin told me she liked it that way.

Likewise, I held back from informing her that she was on my land, though I happily shared tales of local legends and history.

We sat side by side, and her elbow grazed mine. I glanced to find her gaze on the point we touched.

The warmth of the open fire gave me the excuse to grab the neck of my jumper and haul it over my head.

Around us, the ladies stared, taking in my tattooed biceps.

Hailey blushed darker. Now, when her arm touched mine, it was bare skin to bare skin.

That tiny touch alone had me enthralled. I'd never felt anything like it.

She was turned on by me, too. I was certain.

Our fierce chemistry had my pulse thrumming, and my muscles ached where I held myself taut, adrenaline eking through my system. If I'd been attracted to her before, this stranger now had me hornier than an old goat.

It was all I could do to keep track of the conversation and not let my rampant hormones take over.

I really needed to get laid.

After another round of drinks, Hailey stood, placing her hand on my shoulder to ease out of the tight space. I shuffled my chair to let her pass, grazing her waist with my knuckles as she moved.

Her gaze caught mine and clung to it.

In a split second, the chemicals in me surged.

She murmured something I didn't catch for the blood rushing in my ears, then left for the bathroom corridor.

I wanted to rise and pursue her. Except I wasn't a hunter

and, though my attraction was rife, acting on it was another thing altogether. We were strangers, and I didn't know how to do the whole one-night stand thing.

Even if this was obvious. Even if any other guy would've been reading the signs and going in for the kill.

I dropped back in my seat and blew out a breath.

Five pairs of eyes looked back at me. The ladies, Hailey's group, chuckled at each other then started chatting again.

The oldest, a shrewd-eyed blonde named Mirabelle, kept her attention on me. Then she flapped a hand. "You young things. Always hesitating and second-guessing. Dear, I have a request. Go and find Hailey, will you? We don't want her getting lost on the way back."

That did it.

With permission granted by a woman who had to be three times my age, I leapt up and strode through the restaurant, past the diners, and down to the quieter part of the bar. A cool stone corridor faced me, empty.

What the hell was I doing? I half turned to leave. Then a door opened, and Hailey emerged.

She'd reapplied her lip gloss. Those pink, full lips quirked at my stare. "Hey."

"Hey yourself."

We watched one another.

"Mirabelle was worried that you'd lose your way," I murmured.

"Sounds like an excuse."

"Aye, it was."

Hailey inched closer. "Okay," she breathed. "Can I admit something? I'm here for just a night, and there's only one thing on my mind. You, since the moment you walked in."

My blood rushed south. "Christ, lass."

"I don't want to be presumptive but I'm pretty sure you're attracted to me, too, right?"

"Very."

"Then..."

I moved in on her the second she reached for me.

I hadn't seen this coming, not in a month of Sundays, but my frustration with my father coupled with the stress of trying to keep our business afloat drove me on. I was beyond fascinated with this woman and needed to get acquainted with her lips.

Luckily, she had the same idea.

Hailey took hold of my biceps as I hooked her waist. Our mouths met in a perfect, hard kiss. Instantly, I walked her backwards, guiding her to the end of the corridor, around a bend where no one else would go. Hailey let me lead, but the moment we were out of sight, she angled her head and dug her fingers into my hair. Ah God, I liked that.

I licked the seam of her lips and gained access to her mouth, stroking her tongue with mine. Hailey moaned, taking the kiss from unexpected to supernova hot.

This was my first kiss in a year. Fuck was I glad to have it.

People had one-night stands all the time, and this was how. They surrendered to pure animal attraction. No questions asked. No playing games.

This was so far from the man I usually was, but I didn't want to stop.

I caged her against the wall and pressed my hips to her soft body, showing her what she'd done to me.

"God!" Hailey broke our mouths apart. "Come upstairs with me."

Her pretty eyes held mine. This was a no-brainer. Yet I paused.

"How drunk are ye?" I asked.

"I've had a few glasses of wine, sure. But that's making this way easier. I want you and you want me. If you're up for this then so am I."

I closed my eyes and surrendered to the moment. "Aye, lass. Back stairs. Let's go."

3

COCKY SCOT

Ewan and I half fell through my bedroom door, mouths locked and fingers twisting in each other's clothes. He made a rude grab of my backside and pressed me into his impressive erection. I melted, my body loosening up in preparation for what was going to be one heck of a night.

This made up for my mistake with the sales rep, and a good, hard screw was the perfect end to my working vacation.

Ewan took a deep breath and released me.

"On the bed," he commanded.

I hopped to do his bidding, my pulse skittering.

He stalked over, the faint light from the open curtains highlighting the fierce need in his expression. Then, he dropped to his knees and reached for my jeans button, undoing it with a flick of his fingers.

"Thank you, Diane," I muttered.

Ewan paused. "What did ye just say?"

"Ignore me." I wriggled my jeans over my ass.

But Ewan sat back, his eyebrows jammed together in a frown. "Diane, ye said. Do ye mean Diane Kudrow?"

Oh shit. I blinked. "Yes. She's my boss. Why do you know that name?"

"I know the name because I'm meant to be meeting with her in the morning."

Oh no. I widened my eyes in alarm. This whole time, I had Ewan pegged as an estate worker or someone in the tourist trade. "You're meeting with her? That's supposed to be someone called Angus McClintock."

He dug his fingers into his hair. "Angus is my da. I'm Ewan McClintock."

Cooler air swirled over my thighs. Disappointed and increasingly embarrassed, I shuffled back on the quilt and dragged my jeans over my butt once more. Sleeping with a contact was a definite no-no. Almost certainly against the terms of my contract. "I'm here in Diane's place. Which means we can't do this."

"Aye, no kidding."

Ewan leapt to his feet and swung a long look over me. "Fuck," he uttered once more then turned on his boot heel and left.

---

*B*right sunshine filled my bedroom, waking me before my alarm went off. Thick-headed, I popped two Advil, rose from the comfortable bed, and dragged my ass to the shower.

Water sluiced down my body and, in flashes, my brain woke, cheerfully replaying my drunken, horny exploits.

Ugh, last night had been both perfect and utterly awkward.

At least Ewan and I had discovered the connection before things went too far.

Still, regret lingered as I readied myself for the day, choosing a nicely tailored suit with flat shoes for the outing. I dried my hair straight and packed my bag. Tonight, I'd be on my way home again, hopefully with a final deal in the bag.

I checked my phone for messages, finding a voicemail from Diane in which she told me to check my email.

I did, skimming the glowing comments she'd given on the write-up I'd sent her for the three places I'd visited already on my trip. A smart hotel on the Devon coast, an inn high up in the Lake District, and a country estate not far outside of London had all got approval.

Pride lifted my shoulders, and I read on.

Hold fire on any more negotiations. We're considering an entire new package for Scotland. A more upmarket proposal that needs further consideration. Think flashy and exclusive. I know you have the final visit at the inn, but we aren't ready to make them an offer now. We'll revisit the idea at a later date.

Shame for the inn. They could be upmarket but not flashy. Charming and rustic was the vibe here. I tapped back my agreement, careful with my words. Making a good impression on Diane was everything when I only had six months to prove myself if I wanted a permanent position in the company.

The next message I read was from Elodie, my aunt.

Hollis is taking us on a surprise holiday! she'd written last night.

I grinned. My uncle adored his wife and doted on their three kids. He worked hard but also took as much family time as he could.

We're going mid-morning tomorrow. Will we get to see you

before we leave? There's something I want to talk to you about. It's better in person.

I checked my flight time and calculated the difference. The only way I could see Elodie face to face was if I got a flight by lunchtime today, which meant leaving soon. It was possible, as Diane didn't want me to make a deal anymore, but it felt rude just up and leaving without giving Mr McClintock the chance to make his case.

Diane would love the inn, even if it didn't fit her plan. What I'd seen so far had been impressive.

I nodded to myself, making a decision. It would be better if I saw everything they had to offer. I'd get extra points for a thorough job, but that meant I wouldn't get the earlier flight.

I don't think I'll make it, I replied to Elodie, adding a sad face emoji.

Elodie, Hollis, and their children were my world. After the damage my parents had wreaked on my childhood, I needed to keep the better half of my family close. Their leaving for a month wrenched my heart. Plus Elodie's news, the something she wanted to talk to me about, had me worried for her.

I glanced again at the earlier flight but closed down my browser. It wasn't happening. I was here to work, and earning my own money was vital to me.

Except, as I readied the last of my luggage to leave, memories of Ewan's firm muscular arms kept coming back into my mind. The way he kissed me. The thrust of his hips and his impressive bulge going exactly where I needed it, before he called everything off.

Nope. I wasn't going there now. The moment was over, and I'd have to return to my romance novels to fulfil my Scotsman fantasy. I lifted my chin and marched downstairs, in business-mode once more.

Unlike last night, the bar was almost empty, a couple of early risers leaving for a hike. The same bartender emerged from the taproom. "Good morning! Can I get ye breakfast or coffee?"

"Black coffee would be awesome. I'm meeting Mr McClintock here at eighty thirty so I'll skip breakfast until later."

The bartender eyed me strangely. "McClintock junior or senior?"

"Senior." I sighed. At least I wouldn't have to face Ewan again.

He handed me my coffee and chuckled then went back to tidying up.

Weird.

I was a few minutes early so I settled onto a barstool, taking a healthy gulp of my drink. Last night, Ewan had been friendly with the man, and with the woman who worked here.

He wouldn't have told them about my proposition, surely. It might explain the wry smile on the bartender's face.

"Hey," I said, unsure of how I was going to phrase the question.

My words trailed off as Ewan, in all his tall, dark, and handsome glory, walked into the bar.

Bang went avoiding him.

An older man strode beside him, a discontented expression contorting his features.

"Where's Diane Kudrow?" the older man barked.

"I'm Hailey LaCroix. I work for Diane and am here in her place. We emailed ahead about the change." I guessed his son, here, for some reason, had told him about the switch, too.

"Old Mac," the bartender said. "Ewan. Either of ye care for a drink before ye set out?"

Old Mac? Yesterday, the cab driver had warned me about this man. What had he said? That he didn't like tourists?

I swallowed and kept my gaze on him.

His rough cheeks took on a purple hue, and he ignored the bartender's question, focusing solely on me. "Hailey who? Diane Kudrow was meant to meet me today. What's her excuse? I call it rude not to keep an appointment once you've booked it. I dinna enjoy being messed around."

"Da," Ewan said, a warning in his tone.

I slipped from my seat, ignoring Ewan and focusing on the man I was here to see. "Mr McClintock, let me explain."

"Why? Looks to me that I dinna require any explanation at all! I expected one woman, and they sent another." He purposefully gave me a beady-eyed once-over. "From all appearances, a wee slip of a lass barely out of school."

My jaw dropped. "I'm twenty-three and more than qualified to assess your land."

"Are ye now!" He planted his hands on his hips and glowered.

I locked my jaw and glared back.

Inside, I was quaking, but he didn't need to know that. Him or his son.

Ewan stepped in front of his father and ducked to meet the man's eyes. "A minute, aye? Outside. We need to talk."

His father blustered some more but allowed Ewan to lead him to the door and out into the fresh air. I blew out a breath and wilted onto my seat.

"I dinna care!" drifted in through the windows, and I peered to see Ewan's red-faced father flapping his arms.

I turned to the bartender. "Yesterday, my cab driver

warned me about Old Mac. He's Mr McClintock, right? That's what you called him."

"Aye. If ye can, ignore everything you're hearing right now. Ewan will be so embarrassed. His da... Well, he has good days and bad days."

I chewed this over and sipped my coffee. Good days and bad days didn't sound great for clients. No one else was in the bar to witness Old Mac's rudeness, but a helpful or kind face made all the difference in some people's holiday experience.

Diane wouldn't stand for Old Mac's rudeness. Which meant I shouldn't either.

If he was rude to someone like Mirabelle, someone who was relying on us to show them a good time and keep them safe, our reputation would be in tatters.

Suddenly, the Cock Bridge Inn lost its shine.

Ewan returned to the bar, his mouth a flat line. "Hailey," he started.

"Ms LaCroix," I corrected.

After last night, I had to draw a professional line.

"Okay. Ms LaCroix. My father won't be joining us on the tour this morning. I apologise for the confusion. This is a family business, and I'll take ye out and show ye what your clients will see. We'll head first to the castle ruins and move on to the battlefield tour. Then to the mountain so ye can see what it's like for skiing come winter. I'll take ye to lunch and show ye the best scenery in all of the Highlands. You've already experienced a night at the inn..." He paused, and his gaze finally touched on mine.

Heat flared in the depths of his dark eyes.

Oh heck.

I stomped down my own surge of lust, though my fingers

tingled as if wanting to independently tangle in his soft brown hair once again.

But this wasn't happening. Any of it. I heaved a sigh.

"Can I ask a question?"

He nodded, still gazing at me.

"Who makes the decisions in your family business?"

Ewan's expression dialled back to bleak. "Currently, my father has final say."

"Right. He's not happy with the fact I'm not Diane, but is he also prepared to expand your reach?"

His shoulders slumped. "Honestly? I thought so, but I'm not sure."

Irritation crept up on me, boosted by the sexual tension that had no place to go. I'd come a long way to be spurned, not only by Ewan, but his father, too. Plus, Diane had made the point that we'd be looking at a higher-end market so it had to be perfect. Perfectly professional.

As pretty as this place was, they clearly had problems.

If I left now and caught the earlier flight, I'd be back on US soil in time to see Elodie and Hollis before they left for their travels. Find out what Elodie needed to tell me.

I stood and summoned a professional smile. "I'm grateful for the hospitality you've shown me but I don't think your business and mine is a good fit right now. Thank you for the offer of the tour. Maybe another time when your company is ready."

Heart thumping, I spun on my heel and raised a hand to the bartender. "Could you please call me a cab so I can return to the airport?"

"Wait," Ewan grumped from behind. "You've come all the way here—"

"You don't need to tell me that. Now I need to go all the way back again."

"If ye just give me the morning…"

"I think it's better if I go."

He planted his fists on his hips and scowled. "Then I'll drive ye myself."

I couldn't bear it. Over an hour in close confines with him would end me. I'd pay the cab driver extra to show me the highlights on the way out of here. "No, thank you."

The bartender chatted on the phone to the cab company, giving us a semblance of privacy.

"Hailey," Ewan said, a demand in his tone. "Are ye leaving because of what happened between us?"

Cocky Scot. "Nope. Your dad, on the other hand, maybe."

"At least take the tour. See what the place has to offer."

Stubbornness had set in. I liked this man and pitied his situation. But this wasn't happening. "I don't think that's a good idea," I said, quieter.

Ewan gave me one last long stare, exhaled hard, then left the bar.

4
—————

IS THAT A EUPHEMISM?

*H*ailey – *Winter*

The phone on my desk trilled for the fiftieth time this morning, but I put on a smile and answered with a chirpy greeting. Across the bright office space, Diane appeared at the doorway to her office. She waved to me and indicated behind her. Her way of telling me to come in once my call was done.

In the three months I'd spent at Kudrow International Travel, I'd spent more time handling client enquiries than anything else, but I hadn't minded. I knew I'd been lucky to get the site visit right off the bat and I was willing to work my way up.

My secret dream was to run my own business, maybe focusing on a niche area rather than big hotels and resorts. But that dream was a long way off. No accommodation owner would trust a woman with barely any experience. I needed years in this job to prove myself.

A few minutes later, I was done with the call and skipping to Diane's door. "You wanted to see me?"

"Ah, yes, come in." She pointed to the comfy white chair

on the opposite side of her desk. "I've been working on a proposal and I need a researcher to fill in some blanks."

I settled into my seat and thumbed at myself. "I'm your woman. Give me the details."

"Do you remember your short visit to Scotland? I mentioned then that we were going to create a custom package. I've had great interest from clients, so the project has been green-lighted."

My insides warmed. Ewan was what I remembered most about the trip.

I cleared my throat. "Fun! What would you like me to do?"

Diane glanced at her screen over her expensive frameless glasses. "I've just emailed you a list of locations and some thoughts on the type of provision we're seeking. Call the land owners and see if they can deliver what we want. This is going to be exclusive but rural and rustic. Quality but with a down-to-earth feel. I'm thinking billionaires who want to go hiking and pretend they aren't wealthy enough to buy the whole country."

Previously, Diane's description of what she wanted had ruled out the Cock Bridge Inn. She'd wanted flashy over rustic, but this changed everything.

My stomach clenched.

"I get it. Farm-to-table products and friendly staff. Nothing officious but a guarantee of a smooth operation."

"Exactly that."

I chewed my lip for a second. "Is the Cock Bridge Inn on our new list?"

"It is. Your write-up helped form this outline. Do you think they could deliver what we want?"

In my brief description of the place, I hadn't mentioned Ewan's dad's outburst. It seemed unfair when Ewan had made the point it was a family business where he was working on the decision-making. We weren't ready to make an offer, so it had been a moot point. For all I knew, they could've changed up their business model a week later. I hadn't wanted to scupper their chances.

Particularly not when I felt bad for how I'd run away from the place.

"The inn itself is perfect for what you've described, and though I didn't get to go on their tours, the ladies staying there did, and they loved it."

Diane gave a curt nod, her interest already lost to her screen. "Call them up and work through the list. Get their proposal."

"Sorry. One last question. Is there another trip in the planning? I'd love to put my name down."

For this, I got a quick smile. "I'll bear that in mind. I've yet to decide on how we'll run the field visits. It will depend on how strong the proposals are."

Back at my desk, I opened the email as fast as my fingers could click my mouse. There, against the listing for the Cock Bridge Inn, was Ewan McClintock.

I stared.

Ewan. Not Angus, his father.

A quick search on their website and social media gave me the same clue. Ewan headed up their presence and was listed as manager.

His email address practically screamed at me.

Looking back on the evening I'd spent with him, and the more painful following morning, I wished I'd been kinder. But my own selfish needs had taken over, and I'd returned to the States in time to hear Elodie and Hollis's news—they were expecting again. They already had three kids, my beautiful little cousins, and now a fourth was on the way. A tiny surprise for them but very welcome.

Not for the first time, I sighed wistfully at the difference between their babies' upbringings and mine. My mom died of a drug overdose when I was tiny, and my dad was in and out of jail. I was barely double figures when Hollis took me in, recruiting Elodie as my nanny before he fell in love with her and married her.

I was so very lucky with them.

I drummed my fingers on my desk. Like me, Ewan had parental issues. He didn't deserve to be penalised for that.

With vigour, I typed out a friendly email, outlining the needs of Kudrow International Travel. But before I pressed 'Send', I added a personal note to the bottom.

It had to be bland, as anyone could read my business emails, but I couldn't resist sending it.

Mr McClintock – I wanted to thank you again for your hospitality in the fall. I really enjoyed my stay. I think about it often. Hailey.

Then I got on with researching the rest of the list, pretending my heart didn't skip a beat every time my email binged.

---

*B*ut by the time we shut up shop, no reply had come. I waved goodbye to Diane and the other three members of staff and stepped out into a frosty Manhattan evening. As always, Midtown thrummed with busy folks heading home or out for dinner. With thick coats and scarves to protect against the frozen air, they put their heads down and charged in herds.

I had a standing invitation to Thursday night dinner

with my family, but I didn't make it out to Connecticut as often as I liked. Tonight was a go, so instead of turning my cute kitten-heeled boots to the subway and home, I peered into the night for my uncle's car service.

A horn tooted, and I grinned then stepped to the curb. A very nice town car eased out of the traffic and came to a halt, Elodie, my beloved aunt, flapping at me from the back.

"Eek!" I clambered inside with her, the cosiness of the car as warm as Elodie's hug. "This is a surprise!"

"Hollis had to come into Manhattan for business, so I tagged along. He's still in a meeting now, so I came to fetch you."

"Where are my cousins?" It was strange seeing Elodie without a gang of small people around her.

"With the nanny. Sorry to say, but we'll be late home because of Hollis so we're staying in the city for dinner. You and I are going to a fancy restaurant, and your uncle will join us when he's done."

A small blip of disappointment registered, but I soon dismissed it. As much as I adored hanging out with my ten-year-old boy and seven-year-old twin girl cousins, I valued my time with Elodie and the chance to have an adult conversation.

There was a matter I'd been ducking. Maybe I could air it with Elodie tonight.

I rubbed my hands together. "Tell you what, why don't we go back to the apartment and we'll bake a lasagne together? It'll be like old times."

"Done deal!"

The driver knew the way, as I lived in Hollis and Elodie's old Park Avenue apartment, which had been Hollis's bachelor pad, and the place I'd moved to after my father's incarceration.

I shivered, bad memories disrupting my happiness. Yeah, I didn't want to go there with that conversation tonight. It would wait. Instead, I broke out in chatter about my work and Elodie's pregnancy.

In thirty minutes, we were pulling up outside the exclusive residential block. Then we had our meal underway. Elodie had taught me to cook and had some kind of magic touch when it came to turning ingredients into divine dishes.

We were partway through making the white sauce when my email binged. I slid a glance at my phone.

Elodie was busy, and stirring the sauce was a one-woman job. Surely it wouldn't matter if I checked?

I collected my phone from the counter and glanced at the incoming email. Oh God. It was a reply from the hot Scot.

Ms LaCroix, I'm glad to get your message and will prepare a response by the end of the week. Thank you for considering us.

Yours, Ewan McClintock

My heart sank at his business-like tone. What had I expected, a flirty exchange on my office email?

Then, before my eyes, another message appeared.

In reference to your note, I have, too. But that's a separate topic of conversation. Text me here if you want to discuss further.

Below, he'd given his cell number.

I stared. It was an invitation to talk in private. He was being professional but cocky at the same time, wanting to take the chat away from prying eyes.

Which meant a whole bunch of interesting things.

Without dwelling on the matter, I saved him as a new contact then opened a text.

Hailey: Hey, it's Hailey.

I hit 'Send' then held my breath.

"Earth to Hailey?" Elodie waved a sauce-dipped spoon. "Who are you texting? Oh my God. It's a boy, isn't it?"

I gave an unladylike snort. "I'm twenty-three. I don't date boys."

She dropped the spoon back into the saucepan, her eyes wide in delight. "A man, then! Tell me everything. Is it serious? How did you meet? Does he live in the city?"

"Oh no." I pocketed my phone and made the sign of the cross with my fingers, as if she were the Devil. "I'm not making that mistake again. Every single boyfriend I ever had was scrutinized to death by you and Uncle Hollis. You can meet the man I intend to marry the day before my wedding. That's it."

Ewan wasn't anything to me—I'd known him for all of one evening—but my family were overprotective, bordering on nosy, and boundaries had to be maintained.

Elodie smirked and gestured for me to help with the last job of constructing the lasagne from its various parts. Rich Bolognese layered with noodles. The creamy sauce. Spinach. Mounds of cheese. By the time it went into the oven on a timer, I was salivating.

A key in the door announced Hollis's arrival, just as my phone bleeped from an incoming text. I silenced it with a flick of my fingers and waved at my uncle as he appeared at the end of the hall. He shed his icy peacoat and greeted me, but his gaze sought his wife, as it always did.

I let them have a quiet reunion and scanned my message.

Ewan: Which part of the visit stayed with ye the most?

I pursed my lips and tapped a fast reply.

Hailey: Meeting Mirabelle, of course. What about for you?

His response came in a flash.

Ewan: Is that a euphemism? If so, meeting Mirabelle blew my mind, and I haven't thought of much aside from meeting Mirabelle in two months. In fact, I'm lying in my bed thinking on the subject right now...

Holy cow.

My jaw dropped, and it was only Hollis clearing his throat that brought me back into the room.

"Huh?" I said eloquently.

"I asked if we could have a chat." Hollis's gaze dropped to my phone.

Cheeks no doubt flaming, I shoved the device out of sight. "Now? I mean, sure!"

He gestured to the living room, and we filed in, taking seats on the white cube sofas.

My uncle blew out a breath. "Are you aware your father's jail term is almost up?"

Oh. That.

My stomach tightened. "I am. A message came from the jail a few weeks ago."

Hollis's lips twitched, and I knew he was disappointed I hadn't talked to him about it. He and I hadn't known each other when I was little, so he carried a constant regret that we weren't closer. His brother went to jail, and I arrived on his doorstep. Instant baggage to his singleton life.

"He wrote to me, too," Hollis said. "I want to talk to you about how we help him. Settling into a new life could be a challenge."

"What were you thinking?"

"I'd set him up in an apartment and find him a job. Give him one, if needs be."

I twisted my fingers together. "Nice of you."

"How do you feel about it?"

"Which part? He's been in jail for twelve years. I don't really know him."

"He's your dad—" Hollis started.

Elodie pressed her husband's knee. "The question Hollis has is over where we locate your father. Here, in the city, or in a smaller community. Maybe closer to our home."

"Have you asked him?"

"We want to get your view first."

The fact was, I had no desire to see Dad anytime soon. He'd been borderline negligent when he had me in his care, and since going to jail, he rarely got in touch unless he needed money.

Christmases. Graduation. He missed every single one.

Worse was the fact that he'd been absent for most of my milestones when he'd actually been in my life, too.

The food was nowhere near done, but I leapt up. "He can decide where he wants to be. It makes no difference to me. I'm going to make a salad to go with dinner."

I left my kind, loving relatives on the couch and escaped to the kitchen where I could hide away. Someday soon, I'd have to face my father, but until then, I was happy to continue pretending he didn't exist.

* * *

*L*ater, in bed, I recalled the conversation I'd been having with Ewan and returned to the thread. He'd sent a follow-up message, and I scanned it eagerly.

Ewan: Okay. From your radio silence, I came on too strong, aye? Apologies, Ms LaCroix. I can't seem to get it right with you. Consider me rebuked. Goodnight, lass.

It was late. Too late to continue chatting with a man in a time zone five hours ahead of mine. Yet still, I replied, buoyed by the wine I'd drunk to accompany my junk TV binge after Hollis and Elodie left.

Hailey: I had dinner with family. Don't be rebuked. Unrebuke yourself and tell me what happened next with your evening in bed with Mirabelle. In detail.

No response came, but I grinned, snuggled into my soft sheets, and settled in to dream about Scotland.

5

THE SEXTING THING

*E*wan

In haste, I jogged the lane to the row of old cottages down the track from the inn. Ahead, Briana, my cousin, hustled, an iPad in hand and a fierce expression made of determination. We had at most an hour before Da arrived and needed a solid plan.

Between us, we'd discussed the proposal Hailey's company had made and wanted to go for it. But it would be an uphill battle persuading the older generation.

In the couple of months since Da had agreed to meet Diane Kudrow, Hailey's boss, I'd pushed through more change. Now, Briana and I were decision-making partners in the family business, though Da hadn't given up the reins completely.

He wanted money but no change.

Us younger members wanted our families supported and welcomed any necessary adjustment.

Inside the first cottage, Briana flipped on a light switch.

A jumble of broken furniture faced us.

My cousin sighed. "It's a mess."

"Aye, but the roof is solid, and no damp gets through these walls." I gave them a thump for good measure and paced across the room.

Then I talked my cousin through the idea of turning the row of pretty cottages into boutique rentals. Impeccable decoration, meals served at the bar or the holidaymakers could cook for themselves from a hamper we'd supply. It added a good number of extra beds to our setup and balanced out the offer I intended to make to Kudrow International Travel.

Hailey's company.

Her message sent in the wee small hours of the morning had sent my mind into overdrive. I had an adrenaline rush every time I remembered our kiss. Our pursuit to her bedroom.

In two months, I hadn't looked at another woman.

"This is going to be a hard sell." Briana poked at the iPad screen. "The theme you want isn't going to be cheap. I can already hear your da's outrage when we talk about the thread count of sheets and bespoke carpentry."

I pulled a face and checked the time. "We have fifteen minutes to agree how to present this to him. I'm going with the income we'll make first, then slide the investment figure in after."

"As good a plan as any." She cocked her head. "This is the same company that pretty American worked for, aye?"

I rolled my eyes. "Her name's Hailey."

A knowing, teasing grin appeared on Briana's face. I about-turned and marched outside.

"Can ye call her up and ask for help?" She chased me back up the track. "Maybe do a wee bit of flirting with her to get us an edge?"

It was uncanny how close to the mark Briana had got. I

wasn't about to play Hailey for an advantage but I was down with the sexy texting.

"Mind your own business," I called back. "And get your game face on. We're going in."

***

At midnight, I finally made it to my bed, weary from the day but with a buzzing brain. Incredibly, my father hadn't turned down the idea of catering to the high-end market. Approaching with the income potential first had pound signs in his eyes, and I'd got what I wanted: permission to negotiate on behalf of the family. All I needed to do was write up the proposal and send it in to Hailey's company.

Speaking of whom…

I reached for my phone and brought up her last message then wrote my own.

Ewan: How about I tell ye another tale. One where a man met a woman, liked her, kissed her, and took her upstairs. One where they weren't interrupted.

The dots to tell me she was responding appeared immediately.

Hailey: Just getting home from Pilates. Give me more.

Ewan: Are ye hot and sweaty? Getting into the shower?

Hailey: Wouldn't you like to know?

I grinned and adjusted myself in my boxer shorts—the only clothing I liked to wear in bed. Just as in our first meeting, texting Hailey was easy. No front, just pure, amused attraction.

Ewan: Aye. With details. I'll tell you mine if you tell me yours.

Hailey: Water's hot. I'm going in. When I get out, I want a long (very very long) message from you.

Ewan: Got to tell ye, the idea of you naked under running water is driving me wild.

No answer came. She was showering, naked, oh fuck.

My cock hardened. If you didn't ask, you didn't get.

Ewan: I was on the floor, removing your jeans. This time, I got them all the way off, your underwear, too, leaving ye bare for me.

A moment of concern passed over my consciousness. I'd never done the sexting thing before. And though Hailey and I had been down for a one-night stand, I still didn't know her well.

I wished I did. I'd liked the small glimpse of her I'd gotten. Her kind ways, her professional side, her smokin' body.

Hailey: I showered fast. You need to keep going. What will you do with me next?

Ewan: Put my mouth on you.

Hailey: Talk me through that...

Ewan: What are you doing right now? Give me a visual.

Hailey: On my bed, wrapped in just a towel.

Ewan: Lose the towel. Touch yourself.

A decadent thrill replaced my worry. This short conversation was the sexiest thing that had happened to me since...Hailey.

Hailey: I need to know you're doing this, too.

I swallowed at her vulnerability and took a snap in the dark room, the flash lighting up my body. Just my abs with my arm leading out of the shot.

Ewan: Here. I'm alone in my house. Just ye and me.

Hailey: Damn. Wish I'd got a chance to explore you more.

Ewan: Do it now. What do ye want me to do?

Hailey: Stroke yourself.

Ewan: Doing it, sweetheart. Slide your hands down your body. Tell me what you feel.

Hailey: I'm wet from texting you.

Holy shite. I pumped my shaft, picturing Hailey's sweet curves. I badly wanted a picture from her, but it seemed a lot to ask for our first time of sexting. My balls tightened with a warning. The mental image of her was potent enough to push me to the edge.

My phone buzzed, and a photo loaded.

Hailey's fingers crooked over her core.

Well, fuck. A wave of horniness took me under at the dirty image, and I dug my shoulders into the bed, working my cock hard in solid strokes.

With my other hand, I tapped out a message.

Ewan: Sexiest thing I ever saw. Make yourself come for me. Do it now.

Then I stared at her picture and fucked my hand in a frenzy.

Hailey: Fuck! Okay. Coming.

My own orgasm hit me like a steamroller. I closed my eyes and let the hot lashes land on my chest. My brain scrambled, and it was a minute before I could see again to focus on my phone. No reply had come in. I took the initiative, hoping that had been as hot for the American lass as it was for me.

Ewan: I went blind for a second there. Need to clean up now. Fuck, woman. That was something else.

Dots appeared, then vanished, then returned. I'd washed myself down and climbed under my sheets by the time the answer came.

Hailey: Yeah. You can say that again.

I wasn't about to let this go weird. Sure, the sexting had been awesome, but I wasn't done chatting.

I grabbed a picture of myself stood in front of the mountains that made up the backdrop to my home. Briana had taken it to use on our website, but I hadn't uploaded it yet.

Hitting send, I added the caption.

Ewan: Here, in case you forget my face now you've seen my muscles.

A couple of minutes later, my phone lit. A photo of Hailey on a busy Manhattan street. Snuggled in a tailored, woollen coat, she beamed for the camera, her fair hair curling around her collar.

Hailey: My aunt took this of me last month.

Ewan: You're gorgeous.

No further response came, and I closed my eyes and drifted to sleep. Satisfied, intrigued, and very much liking this new game I'd found.

6

GO FOR IT!

*E*wan

All week, I worked solidly on renovating the cottages. At age sixteen, instead of continuing with an education that didn't fit my practical mind, I'd apprenticed at a furniture maker's, learning how to handle wood. My skills would save us a bundle on kitting out the rentals, though I had to hire in help for plastering and stonework.

Every couple of hours, I'd stop for a break, send a message to Hailey, and read through her replies. We fell into easy communication. She was an early riser, though it was still eleven AM my time before she'd come online, a fact I teased her about.

I learned that she was on probation in her travel agency job for several more months, and striving to make a good impression.

On my side, I told her how I was an only child but the oldest of sixteen cousins.

We didn't mention the proposal I was almost ready to submit. Nor did we get down and dirty again with a sexting session. Either I had a late night with work or she had dinners to go to or was meeting up with friends.

Still, my heart leapt whenever my phone buzzed, and I didn't even mind Briana's tease on how distracted I'd become. It was true. Hailey crept into my consciousness, and I was well on my way to having a pretty significant crush on her. A lass that lived thousands of miles away.

Heh. At least this lass couldn't leave me for the big city like my ex had—Hailey already lived in one.

By the time the weekend came, I had the first cottage cleaned up and a new kitchen built. We brought in furniture and staged a photoshoot to add the pictures to the proposal for Hailey's company.

When they signed us up, we'd commit to buying every expensive fitting we needed. If they didn't, we wouldn't have made a poor choice.

But once the shoot was done, I had a dilemma. I wanted to fine-tune it to make sure it hit the mark, but the obvious person to call was Hailey and that seemed a conflict of interest as we'd struck up a friendship, of sorts.

I brought up my chat with Hailey and dashed out a message.

Ewan: Do ye think it would be okay if I contacted your manager? I want to make a good impression and land this deal.

Hailey: Great idea! She likes people who take the initiative. Go for it!

Permission granted, I sat in my comfortable leather office chair and dialled her boss.

"Diane Kudrow. How may I help?"

"Ms Kudrow, it's Ewan McClintock here. A couple of months ago, ye were in contact with my father. We're preparing a bid as we speak to work with ye. I wondered if ye had a minute to chat?"

My muscles tightened, and I stilled myself, forcing my system to calm. We needed this deal.

"Ah, of course." Diane's voice brightened. "Hailey mentioned that we were to expect a proposal from you. How's that going?"

Ignoring my surge of interest at Hailey's name, I glanced at the notes I'd made on my jotter and launched into a confident spiel. I wanted Diane to know what to expect before my email landed, and to gauge her reaction. By the time I'd listed the finer points of our offer and explained how I was heading it up, not Da, she was making sounds of approval.

"I'll look forward to seeing the presentation next week," she said.

"They're being presented?"

"I have two business partners, so we're spending Friday morning reviewing the submissions. If the applicant can't attend, like yourself, then Hailey will be standing up for you."

I mulled that over. In person, anyone would have an advantage. My competitors, whoever they were, would be there to answer questions and add a depth I couldn't even hope to from a distance.

My phone call was nowhere near enough. Plus, Hailey had said Diane liked people who took the initiative.

"I'll be attending in person," I said, the words coming from nowhere, pounds signs racking up behind my eyes at the flight cost.

"We'd be delighted to have you."

We wrapped up the call, and I stared at the office walls, wondering how the hell I was going to convince Da to stump up for my pricey trip.

Then my emotions doubled down because, holy crap, I was going to see Hailey again.

7

GOD, A KILT!

*H*ailey

Diane called from her office at the same second a message landed from Ewan on my phone. Dammit. He'd have to wait a second.

"You didn't mention the Cock Bridge Inn representative was coming here." She gestured to her seat. "Mr McClintock just called. I must say, I'm impressed with his initiative. He's a better fit for us than his grouch of a father."

"Oh! I didn't know." My pulse raced.

Ewan was coming here? I badly wanted to see him again, but shit, I couldn't flirt with him. One hint of inappropriate practice, and Diane had every reason to sling my tush out the door.

My boss chatted on about the preparations, all of which I had well in hand, while my heart sank. I nodded along but, in my head, I was calling things off with Ewan.

Not that we had any kind of relationship, one sexy night aside, but I couldn't stand across the room from him and wait for a sexy glance, or have him reveal how I'd broken the office's no fraternisation rule.

If he won the contract with Diane, that meant a lot of money and bookings going his way.

I was the only one with something to lose here.

The vague worry that he'd started chatting to me in order to improve his chances made itself known. But our talks hadn't been about work. They'd been about sex, TV shows, the weather, Christmas, anything but my job.

Until today when I'd told him to call Diane.

She finished up her instructions, and I dragged my miserable ass to my seat and found my phone. A message waited.

Ewan: Guess who's coming to NYC?

I huffed and threw the phone into a drawer. I had to break things off and I had to do it now.

The following evening, I arrived home from work. Two days of not replying to Ewan had me blue, and I dropped onto my couch without even taking off my coat.

A knock came at the door, and I heaved a sigh and clambered back up to answer it. In a building controlled by beefy security men, very few people could turn up unannounced, which therefore made it a neighbor. I opened the door then yipped to find my best friend, Kelsie, on the other side.

"Oh. My. God!" I swept her into a much-needed hug. "When did you get into town?"

"This morning! I'm staying with my folks while Brandon winds up business, then we're leaving."

"Margaritas?"

"Are you kidding?"

I grabbed her hand and pulled her inside. In the kitchen, we made our cocktails and hugged again.

"When do you head north?"

Kelsie had been my first friend when I'd moved to the city, with her family living downstairs from my uncle's apartment. Without judgement, she helped me navigate the challenge of being a formerly poor kid in a very wealthy new school environment, and I adored her.

Then she'd upped and left for Canada with her military spouse.

"North? Oh no. Our plans have changed. We're going to the UK now. Scotland!"

My heart stuttered, and she carried on, telling me all about the new quarters they'd already bagged at the airbase, upcountry from Ewan's home.

In my mind's eye, I could picture exactly where the airbase was. I'd idly searched the area, more than once, checking out the local provisions for visitors and inventing tour packages in my head. I'd even imagined setting up my own business, linking lots of little inns and rental cottages together into one offer. Run, of course, by me, an independent company. It was my favourite daydream.

I took a long drink, accidentally draining my cocktail. "How long will you be there?"

"Years. I'll miss you."

I giggled as we'd been apart since before college, only meeting up once or twice a year when she was back in Manhattan. We talked all the time, though, and the coincidence of her heading to the place that was constantly on my mind had my head buzzing.

"I met a man from Scotland," I blurted then, at Kelsie's dropped jaw, I grasped my phone and found Ewan's picture.

"Oh, hello Mr. Tall, Dark, and Handsome. God, a kilt!"

"I know! He's lovely. Seriously sexy, too."

"Did you...?" She raised her nicely shaped eyebrows rapidly.

"Almost. We sexted."

She gaped then giggled. "With pictures?"

"Yep. Just a couple."

"Show me!"

I spluttered and shoved her arm. "You pervert."

"I'm living vicariously. Brandon would never do that with me. When we're apart, I always have to talk him through it in great detail, but a picture? No way."

We both burst out laughing.

"Are you going to see him again?" My friend took a long drink.

"Not in the sexy sense. I stopped our flirtation." I outlined the reasons quickly, knowing that question was coming.

At the end, Kelsie sighed. "It makes a good story, even if you can't have him. Such a shame, though. If you married him, I'd have at least one friend in Scotland."

I dropped my forehead to her shoulder and groaned.

Marriage? I couldn't even be in the same city as him and go on a date. Not if I wanted to keep my job.

No, my fast yet intense flirtation with the Scot was well and truly over.

That night, in my bed and long after Ewan's bedtime, I typed out a message telling him that we had to stop talking. For two days, I'd given him the brush-off, but he'd persisted with happy, flirty texts.

It was the right thing to do.

If I lost my job, Dad would come out of prison to an unemployed daughter. An unacceptable position. I had to stand on my own two feet and not live off Hollis's money anymore.

Seeing Kelsie tonight, the woman who had helped me don my layer of respectability when the other kids in school would've treated me like trash, only firmed up my thoughts.

For once and for all, I would prove I was nothing like my father. I had to for the sake of my sanity.

8

SNOWPOCALYPSE

*E**wan*

My cab trundled through the morning traffic, skyscrapers soaring either side of our route. Horns blared, people swarmed.

I was a fish out of water in the city. I'd been to Edinburgh and London, but they had nothing on New York City. The endless grey buildings went on and on, no natural landscape in sight, the river aside.

How could anyone want this over mountains and burns? Steel and concrete against the glory of Mother Nature? I mulled over the decision my ex had taken. I didn't miss her anymore, but nor did I understand the draw. Not in the slightest.

That call of the wild was part of my presentation. The remote splendour of my homeland would soothe the hardest city lover's soul. Hikes and tours in the day, luxury accommodation with tasty meals in the evenings. Who could want more?

The second but no lesser aspect of my anticipation was

in seeing Hailey. She'd given me the heave-ho, but I was ready to get our flirtation back on track.

Out of sight of her manager, of course.

I understood her logic and respected it.

Seeing her alone was going to be a challenge. I was only here for the day, my flight taking off at nine tonight—a detail Da insisted on to avoid the expense of a hotel room. But that left several hours to kill after I'd made my case.

The cabbie peered up at the sky. "Weather's coming in. We got snow forecast for tonight."

"Aye?" I followed his gaze to thick clouds.

Back home, they'd carry a slight tinge of orange, giving the heads-up of the storm to come. Here, a chill held the air when I'd disembarked the plane, but I'd welcomed the bite, needing to wake up after hours dozing upright in the narrow seat.

Maybe the threat of snow should worry me. It didn't, though. Excitement kept me cheerful.

We pulled up outside the agency, and I tipped the driver, as that was a thing here, I'd read, and then it was show time. I straightened my tie and inflated my chest with an inhale of polluted air, then I strolled inside the place that could make or break my family's fortunes.

*T*wo hours later, and I was on a roll. I'd presented the proposal as expected, but my time had long been up and I was still here, answering questions and being as charming as I could.

Across the room, four people nodded along to my tale of the standing stones on our land. I glanced at Hailey. When

I'd arrived, she'd greeted me formally, but not made eye contact.

I'd played along, keeping my cool, but I'd sent her the occasional look, when I was sure that no one else could see. A cocky lick of attention that let her know I was still game for us.

Diane tapped her knee. "It's incredible, and I wish I had time to hear more, but we still have one person to see and we've kept them waiting. Thank you for coming all this way, Mr McClintock."

"Ewan, please."

"Ewan. Did you have anything you wanted to ask before you leave?"

I thought on my feet. "Only that I'd be happy to host ye in a further site visit. We've made a lot of changes in the short time since Ms LaCroix's visit."

"Thank you. We'll bear that in mind. Hailey, would you mind?" She gestured for her lovely assistant to see me out, and my heart thumped.

I'd done it, presented well, and now I'd get my moment with Hailey, too.

Outside the office, she led me to the door and peered out. "It was nice to see you again. Gosh, it's snowing!"

"I missed ye, too."

Her gaze darted around to the mostly empty office. "Ewan!" she whispered.

"I'm going to a café. Can ye recommend one?"

"Gallagher's, two blocks up. It's my favourite, but no one else here goes there."

"Aye? My flight leaves this evening, so I have the afternoon to kill. Find me when ye take a break. Ye have my number."

Her pretty eyes held mine, then she made a barely perceptible nod.

I badly wanted to lean in and kiss her but instead, I shouldered my bag, gave her a meaningful look, and swung outside.

She didn't leave me hanging. In just over an hour, she was weaving the busy pavement outside the windows. The snow had thickened in the short time I'd been in the city. Fat, fluffy splodges hit the passersby. Icy flakes decorated Hailey's hair as she entered the café. I stood from my booth, hidden at the back, and raised a hand.

Then she was there in front of me.

We gazed at each other, and I soaked in the sight of her lovely face. Pink painted the apples of her cheeks, and she pressed her lips together, clutching the thin strap of her bag. "I can't talk to you about work."

"I didnae ask ye to. I just wanted to see ye again, alone. Let myself stare without worry for your boss."

Her gaze softened. "Thank you for not making our...er, connection, obvious."

"Why would I? No one's business but ours."

I patted the seat, and she perched at the edge.

"Naw," I said and reached for her hip and dragged her closer.

Her flowery scent drifted over me.

My mouth watered.

"Are ye sure your colleagues won't wander in here?"

"No. Actually, that's one of the reasons I came to talk to you. This snowstorm is due to hit hard. Diane and the rest of the managers have already left for home. I'll be closing up the office early."

I peered past her to the door. "It's barely a dusting."

Hailey snorted, relaxing a degree but clearly still wary. "Not in the city. Everyone panics, and the services seize up. They're already saying that flights might be cancelled."

"Ah fuck, really?"

"You might want to book into a hotel. Fair warning, you're in one of the most expensive places for hotels, and they'll book up fast if people get stranded."

I raised a shoulder. That was a problem for later. "Is that the only reason ye came over?"

She looked at me from under her eyelashes. "No. I wanted to apologise, too."

"For ditching me?"

Hailey wrinkled her nose. "Yes."

"I get it. Your job's important. I respect that."

"You aren't angry? Most guys would hate having their pride dented like that."

Though we were sitting side by side, our thighs touching, somehow, this wasn't enough. I turned to face Hailey, my elbow on the table.

"Most men? Do me a favour, don't think about other men when you're with me. Ye have no need to."

She coughed, laughing. "God, you're so cocky. I like that about you."

Then her gaze held mine once more.

Slowly, I took her hand and raised it to my lips for a single kiss to her palm.

Hailey shivered.

Electricity crackled between us.

A waiter arrived at the end of our table. "Can I get you some coffee?"

Hailey snatched her hand back. "Please."

The waiter flipped a cup already on the table and poured her drink from his jug, then topped up mine. "Sorry to say, but we can't offer lunch. We'll be closing soon. This storm is about to hit hard."

"Did they upgrade it? I thought it was coming in later this afternoon." Hailey reached for her phone.

The waiter clucked his tongue. "Temperature's dipping, road's already slick. We're expecting nearly a foot of snow by then. They're calling it Snowpocalypse."

I snorted, but Hailey's eyes widened.

"All flights cancelled," she declared. "Every one."

"Doesn't surprise me."

Another customer called, and the waiter left Hailey and me alone.

"I'm stuck here, then," I said, low. Oddly, the idea didn't concern me, despite having no clothes beyond the jeans and t-shirt I'd worn on the plane, but I'd need to find a place to sleep. "Can you suggest somewhere to stay that won't break my credit card?"

"I have a couple of ideas." Her gaze darted to her phone again as a message landed. "Ah, the office is empty. Sarah, the last woman standing, has fled, too."

"Do you need to go back there?"

A glance around showed me the café was almost empty now. People hustled on the street, and a sense of urgency filled the air, as thick as the falling snow.

"I do. I take my laptop home on the weekends so I'm ready to help if clients need advice or if Diane calls."

"Subway's out," one of the other waiters hollered.

Hailey groaned. "Getting home is going to be fun. I'll never get a cab in this weather. What a day to wear heeled boots. Oh, what am I doing? You're stranded, and I'm complaining about my shoes."

"It's a valid worry. Let me escort ye, then we can talk hotels." I drained the last of my coffee refill and gestured for Hailey to stand.

"I live over an hour's walk away," she grumbled but she eased herself from the booth and gazed at me.

"I'm from the mountains. Walking an hour in snow is my bread and butter. Stick with me, sweetheart. I'll get ye back safe."

"Thank you." Her eyes brightened, and colour returned to her cheeks. "I have a crazy idea but I'm pretty sure you're going to say yes."

"What's that?"

"You can stay with me. I have a guest bedroom. Walk me home and it's yours."

Christ. My heart beat out of time. I'd hoped for a chance to get our flirtation back on track. Now, we'd be spending the night together.

Separate beds, perhaps, but the same space.

I'd never been so glad for a wee spot of snow. I grinned, and Hailey's mouth curved, too.

Then we were ducking our heads and running out into the weather.

9

F-F-FINE

Hailey
A quick launch into the office gained me one laptop and a pair of sneakers I'd forgotten I'd stowed in the back room. Thank God, because the sidewalk was treacherous, and Ewan had saved me from slipping twice already.

I packed up my laptop bag then locked the office door, more than aware of his gaze on me as I keyed in the security code. Ewan waited a few doors away, just in case for some random reason Diane had to check the security cameras and saw me leaving with him.

Not that she'd see much through the blizzard. Snow pelted me, and I jogged to Ewan. He looped a casual arm around my waist, and we took off together like I was made to fit in his arms.

"I live on Park Avenue. We'll stay on Fifth all the way past the park. It'll take us over an hour in this."

"Nae problem," was the confident reply, and I put my faith in the knowledgeable Scot.

The chilled air, and the pace we kept up stopped most of

our conversation. But Ewan's grip on me didn't let up. Underfoot, the snow piled up, making an instant, churning mire. It wasn't the fun version of snow, where you could take time and pack snowballs to throw. It had come out of nowhere, bringing a bitter chill with it.

Around us, people in smart suits and slippery shoes did their best to get to wherever they were going, but the farther we went, the heavier the snow fell. By the time we reached Central Park—barely thirty minutes into our trek—I was shivering, my usually adequate winter coat not up to the job of keeping me warm.

"Ye okay?" Ewan asked.

"F-f-fine." My teeth chattered.

Ewan peered at me. "You're not. Your lips are blue. Raise your hand."

My feet had turned to two blocks of ice, and my fingers hurt. My arm quaked as I lifted it.

"This isn't going to work." He planted his hands on his hips and glared at the road.

Fewer cars than I'd ever seen trundled by.

Then Ewan stepped out, right into the path of a cab. It slithered to a halt, and the driver leaned on the horn.

"What are you, nuts?" the driver called.

Ewan ignored him and thumped on the back window.

"Hey, pal, you're taking up one space, but there's seat for three. My lass is half frozen, and if ye don't let us share, it'll be on you if she's harmed. What kind of man would that make ye?"

The door opened, and a businessman poked his head out. Ewan didn't wait. He dragged the door wider then held a hand out for me. I took his fingers and followed him into the car, the businessman spluttering complaints as he moved over. This broke all kinds of city etiquette, I dimly registered, but also, I didn't give a flying crap. Ewan was right. The temperature drop was hurting me, and I needed to get home.

"Get moving, man." Ewan tapped the glass, and the complaining driver moved on.

I closed my eyes, ice melting through my thin pant suit and soaking my feet. Ewan's arm found its way around me once more, and he cuddled me, murmuring sweet nothings.

A short while later, the car slowed, and I opened my eyes to find us near home. "Here's good," I muttered, my jaw still aching from where I'd been shuddering.

I tried to grab my purse, but Ewan gave me a look and handed the driver his card. The businessman harrumphed and said it was on him, and neither of us argued, giving thanks for the ride share.

Gripping Ewan's arm, I directed him across the road to the lovely white-stone building where I lived. The calm of the lobby was bliss and the front desk vacant, so we stepped into the elevator and traveled all the way up.

My icy blood started moving again, and I managed the door key on the first try.

If Ewan was impressed that I lived in a penthouse on one of the most exclusive streets in Manhattan, he didn't show it. But his jaw dropped when we entered the apartment and walked the marble hall to the sunken, minimalist living room. With floor-to-ceiling views over a snowy Central Park, the effect was breath-taking.

"Jesus," Ewan uttered, his thick coat already in his hand.

I unceremoniously plonked down on the couch and plucked at my jacket buttons. "I had the same reaction when I first came here. I was a kid from the wrong side of the tracks and I felt like a pauper showing up." I added the needed explanation. "This is my Uncle Hollis's place. He brought me here when… When I needed a home. He lives with his family in the country now."

Ewan turned to face me and noticed my struggles. "Here." He knelt on the fluffy rug and helped me shed my coat. Now indoors, I was too warm, though my skin was still icy.

Next, Ewan slid off my sneakers, taking my soggy socks with them. He curled his fingers over my toes, and all I could do was watch him.

"Ye should get in the shower." His voice came out gruff.

"You should, too," I said. No matter how hardy the man was, he must be chilled to the bone. Then I blinked. "Oh God. That wasn't meant to sound like an offer to join me."

"No?" His eyes lit in delight, and I couldn't help my grin.

"I'll show you to the guest room. Do you have a change of clothes?"

"Aye, lass."

Despite my near-freezing, his casual use of the word 'lass' sent heat through my body, pooling at my core.

I wobbled upright and padded to the hall. Ewan followed to the guest bedroom.

Then he stepped into my space.

Face to face, he was a head taller than me, and I raised my gaze to find his burning.

"This is your room," I said on a breath.

Slowly, he took my waist and brought our bodies together, and his mouth landed on mine for a quick, warm, and far-too-chaste kiss.

"Thank ye for bringing me home with ye."

I could've given excuses. Finding a hotel today would've been a nightmare for him, and my guest bed was there and ready to be used. But I only nodded, really wanting another warm press of his lips.

Ewan watched me for a moment then gave a small huff and turned to enter the room. He went straight for the bathroom, leaving the door open, then reached back and pulled his shirt over his head.

Those biceps... His tattoos.

I yipped and reached to close the guest room's outer door then hurried to my bedroom.

I knew what I was doing, bringing him here. I'd wanted Ewan from the moment I'd seen him but hadn't counted on just how strong that longing would become.

Tonight was going to be a whole heap of fun. Once I'd defrosted.

***

In my bedroom, I shed my damp clothes and got myself under hot water. Knowing Ewan was doing the same next door, naked, had my skin tingling, but I rushed through my bathing and dressed again in a soft pink sweater and yoga pants.

Usually with men, I put on a front. Armor, maybe. Aunt Elodie had taught me to be cautious over who I trusted. Before she married Hollis, she'd worked for a private detective agency entrapping cheating husbands, so she knew her stuff. She'd advised me to look at how boyfriends treated their mother and sisters, and how many long-term friendships they'd managed to keep.

What did I know about Ewan? I'd seen him joke with his cousin, Briana, and he seemed to be at the very heart of his community.

Couldn't get much more solid than that.

I swung open my door. The guest bedroom was already vacant, so I wandered to the kitchen.

In jeans that hugged a very nice backside, Ewan pondered the appliances. "Where's your kettle?"

"Don't have one."

"How do ye boil water for tea?"

I raised a shoulder, my humour returning. "Microwave?" His outraged face had me spluttering a laugh. "We're a nation of coffee drinkers. Tea is for when you're sick."

Ewan muttered and filled two mugs from the faucet and placed them in the microwave. I rested a hip against the counter and watched him, happily eyeing the way his black t-shirt sleeves stretched over his beefy arms.

I'd bet all that muscle didn't come from a gym. He'd run mountain trails for exercise. Maybe lift logs or rocks instead of weights.

"Do ye at least have tea?" His voice broke my reveries.

"Hmm? Yes! A box of English Breakfast. I'll grab it." I twisted to open a cupboard then extracted a box.

When I turned, Ewan was right behind me.

I held my breath.

"Thank ye," he said, so close.

I tapped the box to his chest and slid my other hand over his firm shoulder and to the nape of his neck. Then I pulled lightly to bring his mouth to mine.

Ewan didn't hesitate. He tossed the box behind me then pressed my body to his. With a bossy move, he took ownership of the kiss, stroking into my mouth with his tongue.

Just like with our first kiss, I melted. His taste did something to my brain, and I blipped out, entirely able to live in the moment in a way I never usually could.

God, this man knew how to kiss. He was heat, and action, and unapologetically masculine. Firm, sexy slides of his mouth. Gentle persuasive pulls that had me demanding more.

"Missed this." He laid his lips on my cheek then below my ear.

I gasped and twisted my neck to give him better access. "Not possible. We only did it once."

"Not in my dreams. I've relived that night many times."

God! I held his face and returned his mouth to mine. Ewan lifted me to sit on the counter and inserted his broad body between my thighs.

In a minute, as he explored my mouth, I was gasping and clinging to him.

The doorbell bing-bonged.

"Ignore it," I ordered and kissed him again.

Ewan's grin derailed me. "Who would come looking for ye? Might they be worried?"

I withdrew a couple of inches, my hand on his chest.

Under my palm, his heart raced. *Good.*

Mine did, too.

"Fine, I'll check," I replied.

Ewan helped me down, his cocky smirk firmly in place, then turned back to his tea-making task while I went to answer the damn door.

Kelsie's worried face greeted me. "You're here! Can you believe that snow?" She stepped forward, unwinding a thick scarf. "I got home and saw the elevator stop at your floor, so I quickly checked on Mom and Dad then came to you."

"Um, Kels?"

"You must have got home in the nick of time. It's a white-out. Like something from a movie." She kept on going deeper into the apartment. "Mom sent me right on up here with an order to bring you to lunch. She was meant to be hosting a group of her girlfriends, except no one else can make it. But my better half is here, so it'll be fun. Are you good to go?"

Ewan appeared at the end of the hall.

With almost comedic timing, Kelsie skittered to a halt.

She glanced back at me, her eyes wide in a devious, delighted expression. "And who might this be?"

"Kelsie, meet Ewan. Ewan, this is my best friend, Kelsie."

She almost skipped over and shook his hand.

"Good to meet ye," Ewan said.

"You're Scottish?" Kelsie said. Then her gaze found mine once more, recognition dawning. "This is the man you were telling me about?"

"Hush!" I closed in on them.

Ewan grinned and stuck his hands under his armpits.

"You should both come to lunch," Kelsie declared. "My husband and I are about to move to Scotland, and I have so many questions." She blew her bangs. "Wait, unless you're busy right now. Dinner is also an option. Assuming you'll still be here, Ewan?"

"Aye, I will."

Kelsie practically jiggled on the spot at that little nugget.

"We can come now," I said quickly.

I darted to my room to change into slacks then hurried back so Kelsie didn't have too long alone with Ewan.

Later, I'd have that chance. With any luck, I'd only had a tiny taste of what this man was capable of.

10

FROM FASCINATION TO DOWNRIGHT DIRTY

*E*wan

Throughout the friendly lunch with Hailey's friends, my lass shot me looks that ranged from fascination to downright dirty. As nice as it was hanging out in company, I couldn't wait to get her home.

"Where in Scotland are ye moving?" I asked Kelsie and Brandon, her hulk of a military husband.

I was a big guy, but he was a beast.

"Moray."

"RAF Lossie?"

The man perked up. "Lossiemouth. That's the place. Did you serve?"

"Naw, but a relative of mine did. Gordain McRae. He trained as a helicopter pilot there. I'm about an hour south into the Cairngorms National Park. When will ye relocate?"

They told me all about their upcoming plans to haul their lives overseas. I listened and felt for Kelsie, as being a military wife couldn't be much fun, but again and again my attention landed on Hailey.

On the flight out, I'd tried to settle what it was that

intrigued me about her. Seeing her now, and kissing her, brought that answer into sharp focus. It was chemistry, first and foremost. I'd felt it when I first saw her. We connected in conversation, too.

Her being blue from the cold earlier had sent me into a spin.

She knocked me on my arse, pure and simple.

Another hour passed before we were able to politely leave. Hailey and I thanked our hosts then walked the hall to the lifts.

At my side, she stared forward.

Energy bristled inside me.

The lift arrived, and we stepped in, waving once more to the kind people who'd fed us, but the moment the doors closed, our cool evaporated.

I spun into Hailey the moment she reached for me. Not wanting to waste any time, I lifted her, and she dragged in a breath then wrapped her legs around my waist.

Christ. Backing her to the mirror, I gave her a furious, needy kiss, in case she had any concern that my passion for her had dimmed. Hailey hummed appreciation and returned my fever tenfold.

At the penthouse floor, I carried her blindly through the apartment and to the sparsely furnished lounge. The stunning view held no interest for me, though darkness turned the city a sparkling grey.

"Ye live alone here, aye?" I placed Hailey on the couch and sat on my haunches.

"Yep."

"Naw expecting anyone else to visit?"

"Nope."

"Good." I reached for the hem of her jumper as she grabbed for mine.

I relented and stripped my top, revealing my bare chest. Hailey's followed. Then her lacy, pretty bra fell away, too. I ogled her high and firm breasts.

She licked her lips and rested back on the cushions. "Jeans, too."

I complied and stripped entirely. With no boxers, I was exposed to her hungry gaze. My cock bobbed under its own weight, and I palmed it.

"Now ye," I almost growled.

Hailey raised her pert backside and wriggled out of the rest of her clothes. There was nothing for it, so I climbed onto the couch, covering her naked, gorgeous body with mine.

Neither of us paused again. Naked, we kissed, urgency in how we clashed.

I ducked and took a mouthful of her breast and loved on her nipple, swirling it into a peak. She dug her fingers into my hair and tangled her legs with mine. Her moan when I pressed my lips to her belly then kept moving south had my blood running even hotter.

I thought after a year I'd be out of practice with this. But no. Hailey's body needed to be worshiped, and I was happy to be her devotee. I'd never been so turned on, and we'd barely started.

At the juncture of her thighs, I spread her legs wider with my palms and dipped to lick her right where it mattered. She groaned, and I did it again, tasting heaven.

"More," she begged.

"Patience." I kissed her thigh then traced a finger over her soaking, bare core and pushed inside.

"God!" Hailey yelped.

I added another finger, stretching her, then bowed to suck her clit.

Hailey writhed under me, urging me on. Her moans grew louder until she bucked and collapsed, her internal muscles clamping on my fingers.

Holy fuck.

I returned to her mouth, and she kissed me through her orgasm.

My cock pulsed with need, and I grinded against her. Hailey waved at the bag she'd discarded earlier.

"Condom. Packet in my bag."

"On it." In fifteen seconds, I'd suited up and was back exactly where I wanted to be.

I set Hailey on my lap, and she rose and got me into place.

"I imagined this so many times," she confided on a whisper.

"I did, too. Alone in my dark room, with ye on my phone. I wanted ye in my arms."

Hailey sank down on me.

We both groaned.

"So perfect." I whispered.

"God, Ewan," was her reply.

Hailey gripped my shoulders and rode me, her knees digging into the cushions. In this position, I could witness the desire etched on her features, and that look... I liked it far too much.

I met her moves with thrusts of my own, fucking her as she worked me. Together, we slowly drove each other wild. Every roll of my hips had her gasping. Each time she crashed down sent sparks flying in my brain.

Her breasts crushed against me, so I played with her, getting all the more turned on until I was almost blind with needing to come.

My breathing came in short pulls. My balls tightened. I

wanted to get her off again before this first round finished but I was too close. I was—

"Ewan!" Hailey threw her arms around me and kissed me, riding out her second orgasm.

I whipped her up and flipped our positions so I was bearing down over her again. Then I took off at a crazy pace, thrusting like a piston.

My long groan burst from me, and I came in head-swimming bliss. I jerked one last time then collapsed down on a soft bed of Hailey.

She giggled and hugged me, breathing as hard as I was. "Better than your dreams?"

"Aye, sweetheart. Unbeatable. Now come here."

We kissed until I was hard again, but Hailey guided me to the shower. Inside, she soaped me up then dropped to her knees to get better acquainted with my cock.

Her hot mouth saw out my second orgasm, but I was gunning for more.

After, when we dried off, the lass eyed me. "Did you just mutter something to the ceiling?"

"It was thanks to the big man for sending the storm. Without that, we'd never have happened, and that would be a travesty."

"You can say that again."

I did, and she laughed, then we took to the bright kitchen to see about a meal. Maybe some aspects of the big city weren't so bad after all.

Or perhaps that was just Hailey.

"How old are you?" Hailey perched on the counter, her bare soles on the cupboard below.

"Twenty-eight. You're twenty-three."

"How do you know that?"

"Ye yelled it at my da."

She snorted. "I did. Sorry."

"Eh. He deserved it."

"Do you have a middle name?"

"Angus. Ye?"

She tapped her chin. "Ewan Angus McClintock. Ridiculously sexy. I don't have one. It's just Hailey LaCroix."

"Okay ridiculously sexy Hailey LaCroix. Try this." I held up a spoonful of sauce, and she tasted it.

"So good! You can cook. Better and better."

"Glad I got stranded?"

Her gaze softened, and she lifted her chin in a 'yes'. Her smile set off a flurry of emotions in my chest. Ones I hadn't expected. I returned to the creamy sauce—ready to be poured over chicken and served with pan-fried vegetables—not allowing myself to dwell too much on how much I liked this lass.

We ate at a glass-topped table perched in front of the huge windows. Here, I took a good look at Hailey's view of the city. The snow fell more gently now and had settled on everything. Few, if any, cars skated down the roads, and the whole place had a peaceful feel, utterly at odds with the frantic rush I'd landed into.

Similarly, Hailey's flat had a minimalist, uncluttered feel. Shiny white surfaces. No handles on any drawers. Very different to my rustic stone-and-wood home.

"Do ye like living here?" I asked.

"Yes and no. My friends are here, and my job, but I spent

the first ten years of my life in a small town. My uncle and aunt live in Connecticut, and when I stay with them and see their kids running around their huge garden, I miss that open space. This," she gestured to the skyscrapers and twinkling lights, "is fine for now, though. I love being able to come home at three in the morning and have takeout delivered in thirty minutes. Or going to the world's best museums and art galleries whenever I choose. When I have kids of my own, I think those priorities will change."

I chewed my last bite of chicken and pondered this. "Ye want kids?"

"Yep. I had kind of a rough childhood and used to find myself obsessing over how I'd do things differently. I had a great therapist for a while, and she helped me turn those negatives into positives. Learning points, you know?"

She had talked about relatives but not her parents. "Can I ask what happened?"

Hailey drained her wine and set the glass back on the table with a click. "Maybe another time. I like having you here and don't want to spoil that by getting us both depressed."

My heart ached, but she was right and it was none of my business. "What shall we do instead?"

She dabbed at her mouth then rose and collected my plate and hers before sashaying to the kitchen. "Ooh, let me think. Lucky for you, I have a very big imagination."

Ah God, I liked her very, very much.

11

THAT THING WE'RE NAW DISCUSSING

Hailey
A hefty, warm arm wound around my waist, and Ewan kissed my neck. His dick pressed into my bottom, and I wriggled against it.

Last night, we'd screwed, watched a movie with popcorn, then fell into bed together. My bed. It had been a long time since I had a guy stay over so I fully intended to make the most of it.

"Grab a condom," I muttered, still barely awake.

Ewan made a gruff sound then rolled away. A foil packet crinkled, then his hand landed on my backside, dragging my sleep shorts down my legs.

He fitted his dick to my core and without delay, pushed home, both of us exhaling with sleepy neediness.

I backed onto him, but this was Ewan's show. He hauled me half onto his chest then thrust into me, taking his leisurely time about it. One hand snaked inside my top to feel up my breasts, and the other went to my clit.

He worked me, slow and easy. His big dick stretched me,

hitting the same spot over and over, and his fingers rolled my nipples or rubbed circles onto my clit.

Sex was a rarity for me. Good sex, a mythical beast.

An orgasm wound in tight coils deep inside my body.

We were at the wrong angle for a kiss, so I brought my fingers to join Ewan, first at my boobs then into the slippery centre where we joined.

"Ye like that? Feeling me fucking ye?" he said.

"Yes."

He growled and moved faster. Even, steady thrusts that had me stilling my efforts to let him do his thing. My body sang, heat rising, and my breathing came hard. I tensed my muscles, pleasure emanating from multiple places at once and blowing my mind.

"Come, lass," he said in my ear.

That had never worked on me before, the order to come on command, but it did now, and I splintered, coming hard before I'd even opened my eyes for the morning. I draped on Ewan, happily boneless.

He clamped my body to his then, in short order, groaned out his own orgasm to the quiet of my bedroom.

I felt every pulse and spasm. Somehow, this was more intimate than it should be. Maybe because I was so relaxed with him.

"Morning, sweetheart." He kissed my hair.

I giggled, my laughter a surprise. "Good morning to you, too."

Then I got my wish to have his mouth on mine again. What a way to wake.

An hour later, we peered from the windows, coffee mugs steaming in our hands. I'd offered to make Ewan the tea we'd missed out on yesterday, but he was willing to try things my way.

Outside, snow blanketed everything, cars left as big white lumps in the vacant streets.

Snowpocalypse had transformed Manhattan to a beautiful wilderness.

Ewan switched his attention to me. "I'm going to go out on a limb here and suggest it's unlikely I'll be flying today."

"Probably not."

That deep-brown-eyed gaze held mine. "Want me to find a hotel?"

"What? Why would you? Is my place not good enough?" I raised an outraged eyebrow.

Ewan's mouth curved into a smirk. "Ye know that isn't what I meant. I dinna intend to outstay my welcome, that's all."

Strangely, I did know what he meant, and I had the strangest urge to bundle him in a hug to set his mind at rest. But doing so would be leaping from a physical to emotional connection, and I knew my limits. Was all too aware how dangerously close I could get to becoming attached to him, and that wasn't happening.

I stepped back, smiling over my mug. "If you cook another meal like last night's, you can stay."

He prowled after me, hotter than a man had a right to be in black boxers and a tight t-shirt. "If feeding ye gets me another day and night with ye, I'm dedicating my life to becoming a chef."

"I like that. Now follow me. I have a plan," I said.

I led him to my bedroom and into the walk-in wardrobe. Once or twice a year, I went skiing in Vail with Hollis and Elodie and had winter clothes that never otherwise saw the light of day.

I lifted a thick jacket from the rack.

Ewan rested a shoulder on the doorframe and nodded approval.

"You're in my city and officially my guest for another twenty-four hours. I'm going to show you around."

Ewan pointed at the pair of skis at the back of the wardrobe. "Can we take those out?"

I spluttered a laugh. "Not everyone can have a mountain in their garden, so nope. We're going to walk to the park. Build up an appetite then come back for lunch and an afternoon nap. Sound good?"

"No place I'd rather be."

Thirty minutes later, we left my building and stepped out into the transformed wonderland. Neighbors I rarely saw were doing the same, gingerly walking in the dense snow and goggling in delight. I'd seen snow here before but nothing like this. The usual bustle of the metropolis had evaporated.

We were in the gap between Thanksgiving and Christmas, and decorations I'd barely noticed now stood out. Lights around doors. Trees in windows with chain-link decorations in arches.

I didn't bother, as it was midway through my school Christmas concert that I found out Dad was going to jail, so the holiday season could go to hell, but I almost admired these now.

Ewan set a confident arm around my back, and we strolled and crunched over the frosty ground together. Over Fifth Avenue, we entered Central Park and headed into the Meadows. Ewan's face lit at the open space, and he jogged away then scooped up snow.

"Don't you dare," I warned.

His snowball whizzed past my ear.

I glared, but he already had another one, packed in his palm. "The first was a warning. Now, it's war."

"Oh yeah?" I scooped my own, dodging Ewan's onslaught.

We threw snowballs at each other like we were kids, until I shrieked at the icy trickle that made its way down my neck.

Next thing I knew, I was in Ewan's arms and falling into a snowbank.

We kissed right there in the middle of the park, and it was the single most romantic moment of my life.

By the time we made it home, my fingers were tingling again. Ewan jogged to make tea, and I rubbed my hands together and fired up my laptop.

"Sorry, but I need to check in with work and return any phone calls."

"Dinna fash. I'll make lunch." He dropped a kiss on my hair and delivered a hot mug of tea to help me defrost.

"Does 'dinna fash' mean don't worry?" I scanned my email.

"Aye."

"Cool! I can speak Scot."

Ewan huffed a laugh, but my attention snagged on a message from Diane.

Sender: Diane Kudrow

Subject: Shortlisting

Dear all,

See below shortlist for the Scottish package tours. We'll move to the next stage over Christmas and aim to have the offer ready for spring sales.

The message continued detailing actions for various people, but I scrolled down, my heart thumping. Though we hadn't once mentioned work, I'd watched Ewan's presentation, and I knew how important it was for him to win the bid.

Cock Bridge Inn

God! His company was top of the list. Top! Diane hadn't mentioned ranking, but this was a good sign.

Ewan strode across the room with cutlery and set the dining table. He gave me a sexy smile, and I ducked back to my laptop and clicked off the email.

I had information he wanted. Could I tell? It would only be a matter of time until he found out as one of the actions was for me to meet with Diane and discuss developing the offers until we had a clear set of winners.

For twenty minutes, I distracted myself, replying to customers, then stopped to eat hot sandwiches with Ewan. After, he sprawled on the couch and gestured for me to lie down with him.

"Soon. I have a few things to finish."

"Don't be long," he mumbled then threw his arm over his eyes and, in a minute, gently snored.

Sleep didn't come for me. I'd ran out of work to procrastinate over, so I put on a quiet movie and curled up at Ewan's feet.

I must have dozed, though, as I found myself airborne in his strong arms. He kissed my forehead and carried me to bed, then we curled around each other and another hour vanished.

The sex, the exercise, it had wiped us out.

Even so, there wasn't a single other man in the world I could imagine being so comfortable with as Ewan.

Late in the afternoon, after we'd woken and he'd gone down on me, Ewan escorted me to the kitchen. He poked around in the fridge and in the cupboards, questioning me over what I wanted.

Pressure ate at me, though.

I watched him, seeing dependent families with their hopes pinned on this visit.

He was so kind, sweet, and hardworking. Generous, and not just in bed, but in everything he did. On the way back from the park, he stopped to help an older gentleman along the sidewalk. The senior had intended a short walk but found he couldn't move so easily in the snow.

Ewan saw him all the way home.

Such a good person deserved only good things.

"So what will it be? I'm impressed with how stocked up ye are—"

"You got shortlisted," I burst out.

Ewan frowned. "What?"

I slapped my hand to my mouth then laughed. "I read an email from Diane earlier. Your inn is top of the shortlist."

His eyes widened. "Fuck!"

"I know!"

Then I was in his arms, and he spun me around.

Our mouths met in a happy kiss.

"This weekend couldnae get any better," he said sweetly. "I've had ye, time off with nothing to do but enjoy your fine self, and now this."

"We can't talk about it." I made big eyes at him.

"Talk about what?" Ewan made a lips-zipped motion then threw away the key.

We both grinned, and he hugged me again, joy in the strength of his hold.

Our happy evening passed with another exquisite meal, a lot more touching, then a good night's sleep.

Morning saw the airports open again, and Ewan lucked out in a seat allocation on an early flight. He left me at the apartment door, a devastating kiss nearly making him late.

He paused at the elevator and fixed me with a long look. "That thing we're naw discussing, go to your manager and beg or bribe your way onto that project. They'll want to do another site visit, aye? Be on that trip. I need to see ye again, and soon. Promise me you'll try."

Those words were the easiest promise I ever had to make, and with that, Ewan was gone.

12

PINING

*E*wan

For two weeks, I toiled, throwing myself into the backbreaking task of fixing up the remaining cottages then starting on the smaller jobs needed at the inn. I could've lied to myself and said my energy came from needing to get the work done before a visit could take place, but the truth was, I missed Hailey.

Hard.

For someone I'd seen in two short hits, I'd formed a connection despite warning myself against it.

"It's Christmas Day and you're still working. Knock it off for a couple of hours, will ye?" Briana poked her head into the office.

Outside my door, the inn buzzed with activity. Every year, we threw a huge dinner for family and friends, plus the occasional customer who needed a home for the holiday. It was almost as big as our Hogmanay New Year celebrations, but this year, instead of drinking it up and enjoying myself, I couldn't settle.

"Aye. Later."

My cousin never listened to a word I said. "Want to talk about her?"

"No. But I'll tell ye the total spend on the refurb. Those contractors we used were pricey."

"They did an excellent job, though." Briana leaned in and made a face of pain as she clocked the figure on my screen. "Holy fuck."

"Aye. It'll be worth it."

"Question: Did ye tell Old Mac that you're courting the Kudrow agency still? I heard him badmouthing them earlier. He's drunk already, so it could be bluster."

"It's all in the paperwork. Besides, he's given us enough control. I'm nae bothered."

As it had done fifty times today, my gaze slipped to my phone. Hailey and I were in daily contact, but I knew this morning might be different. She was waking up at her relatives' home in Connecticut so she could see her cousins open their presents. I'd probably hear from her tonight.

In front of my eyes, the phone lit. Hailey calling.

"Ooh!" Briana's gaze turned delighted.

"Out!" I gestured at her, and she laughed, closing the door after herself.

"Hey, sweetheart!" I answered the call.

"Hey, yourself! Merry Christmas! I have approximately thirty seconds until the madness kicks off but I just wanted to tell you I have a gift for you."

"Ye do?" My heart pounded. I'd had the urge every day to buy something for her and ship it, but at the same time, it felt presumptuous.

Hailey might not think about me the same way I thought about her.

Playing it cool was so far from my natural order, but I was trying.

"Late last night, Diane emailed me. I was on my way here, and then my phone died so I didn't get to message you…"

"Out with it, woman!"

"I'm coming to the UK!"

I shot forward in my seat, my chair rolling on its casters. "When?"

"Four days' time. I need to go see one other place first then I'll be with you on the thirtieth."

"What a gift! Ah God, you've made me so happy. How long can ye stay?"

"Maybe three days. And it's just me, too. Diane visited the third shortlisted place herself recently and wants to spend time with her family. She thinks this is going to be a hardship for me."

We both chuckled then wee voices yelled in the background of her call.

"Here come the kids. Things are about to go crazy here. I'm totally regressing and living the childhood I never had. Pretty sure my aunt has bought us all matching onesies for the day."

My vision summoned a happy, domestic scene with Hailey at the heart of a loving family. "That, I've got to see. Send me a picture, sweetheart. Can we talk again tonight?"

"Yes! Gotta go. Love you! Bye!"

She hung up, leaving me staring at the phone.

Love you.

My heart thumped. It had been a figure of speech, of course. We didn't know each other well enough to have fallen in love.

Except I knew myself.

Another few days in her company, and I'd be a goner.

Which left me with one huge problem. Like my ex,

Hailey was tied to the city. I was tied to my land. Loving someone meant hurting when you were apart. Pining, like I had been for a fortnight. It meant making plans together and picturing a future. How could I do any of that when she was fighting for a permanent job so far away?

13

NO ONE LIKES SURPRISES

Hailey

My first suspicion something was wrong came right before Christmas lunch. In my reindeer onesie—identical to the ones Elodie and my cousins wore, Hollis compromising only enough to wear fuzzy antlers—I set the table ready for our meal.

There were six of us, three adults and three children.

A visibly pregnant Elodie followed me in with another place setting.

She adjusted the furniture, making space for mystery guest number seven, then fussed over a sprig of holly.

"Who are we expecting?" I asked.

Her hesitation gave me pause.

My father's possible early release from jail had been at the edge of my consciousness, yet I hadn't wanted to check. He hadn't called me, so I'd been content to assume he was still inside.

I'd selfishly wanted today to be special so I'd decided to call him tomorrow.

Mystery guest seven had to be him.

Elodie chewed her lip then heaved a sigh. "This was a bad idea. I knew it. Hollis wanted to surprise you, but I knew this would be a shock."

"No one likes surprises," I murmured. "Dad's the extra guest, right?"

"Yes, honey."

My heart sank to my fluffy reindeer slippers.

The doorbell rang.

From the kitchen, my uncle stuck out his head, beaming. "Hailey, could you please get that?"

I adored my uncle so much, and I knew his heart was in the right place. He loved his brother despite the man's shortcomings. I was the reason for that love, I'd long guessed. Hollis had once told me that my father couldn't be all bad because he'd made me.

I didn't agree with the sentiment.

Yet I couldn't be rude to my uncle and aunt. They'd given me everything, and their hopeful gazes only strengthened how I wanted to do right by them.

On slow, regretful feet, I trudged to the door.

On the other side, my father waited.

"Hello, Dad." I stared at the crow's feet around his red eyes. The wishy-washy color of his hair. The emptiness of his expression.

"Hailey. Didn't know you lived in this mausoleum, too."

"I don't. I'm visiting for Christmas."

Empty-handed, Dad shrugged then bypassed me and strode inside, his gaze bouncing from the huge, decorated tree in the hall to the small collection of gift envelopes Hollis had left on a side table—presents for the people who worked for him.

"Stephen, welcome." Elodie swept out and embraced my father. "Merry Christmas! Isn't it wonderful that Hailey's here?" She waved in my direction. "You've been so busy since you've been out, so this is a reunion as well as Christmas."

"What? Yeah." Dad looked me over and produced a faint smile. "When's the food ready?"

Elodie blinked. "If you're hungry now, I can check on the appetizers?"

Dad huffed and stepped into the kitchen, Elodie following.

Wow. Just...wow.

I watched them go then sidled to the table and picked up the envelopes then carried them into Hollis's office. Dad being here was a betrayal, of sorts, I contemplated as I hid the cash-stuffed envelopes in a desk drawer. Maybe not of me, as my uncle and aunt only wanted everything to be okay, but of Christmas, my childhood, and my general happiness.

Dad had barely acknowledged me.

A spike of unhappiness wound inside me, unhappy memories surfacing. Once, when I'd been around seven years old, a friend from a nice family gave me a gift for Christmas. I had no money so couldn't return the favour but I treasured the present to the point that I unwrapped it with care, peeked inside at the three books, swallowed back my absolute delight, then wrapped it back up. I'd placed it under the drawing of a tree I'd made for our living room, treasuring the thought of having a gift to open in the morning.

The next day, Christmas Day, the package had gone.

Dad claimed no knowledge, but it couldn't have walked out on its own. My guess was he sold it to some other drunk in the bar, some degenerate who had forgotten to shop for their own child.

Who would do that apart from a sick, desperate man?

I knew this would be how it went. He was a taker, not a giver. If I wanted a relationship with him, I'd be the one making the calls and reaching out. Letting the mishaps slide. Been there, done that when he was in jail. Got nothing in return.

Today only showed me how real that would be.

Even so, I owed it to my family to at least pretend to give him a chance. I closed the drawer then took off my reindeer onesie, leaving it in the office to be put back on once Dad had gone. Then I pasted on a mask to hide my regret.

In the kitchen, my father rooted around in the fridge while Elodie fluttered around him. He piled cold cuts and sauces on the counter before going back for more.

She'd worked her butt off over the nearly ready meal, and he couldn't even wait?

My cousins stared in horror.

Hollis pressed his lips together and switched his gaze to me. "Are you okay?"

"Fine!" I trilled, though it was a big fat lie.

My uncle's gaze turned thoughtful, no doubt trying to see into my heart. He dropped his tone. "We have a gift for your dad. Would you like to be the one to give it to him?"

Actually, all I wanted was to curl up in bed again. Or get on a plane and fly to Ewan. Anything but pretend all day to be something I was not.

"Of course. It's Christmas!" I forced out. "Family is everything."

I was sure, though, that unless it was something Dad could sell, he wouldn't be grateful even one tiny bit.

A painful dinner came and went, where Dad talked about himself and his needs, all the while swearing liberally in front of the children.

After, he stayed, drinking more than he should and effectively destroying Christmas.

I escaped to my room at the earliest possible moment.

With any luck, Ewan would still be up. I'd pictured him at the inn. Sure, he had a difficult father, too, but I'd bet his day had gone a whole lot better than mine.

More, I wanted him to make me forget in the way only he could.

14

A MAN OBSESSED

*E*wan

Late in the evening, still in my office at the inn instead of my small cottage, I nursed a whisky, alone with my thoughts now my family members had returned to their own homes. Hailey had been on my mind constantly, and I had the urge to fly to her just so we could travel together.

I was a man obsessed.

My phone buzzed, and I snatched it up, ready to spout nonsense I wasn't sure I should be saying. But Hailey's sniff instantly had me on alert.

"What's wrong?"

She took a deep breath. "God, my cloud of doom precedes me. How can you tell I'm upset?"

"Talk to me. What's happened?"

Hailey groaned, and there was a thud like she'd banged her head against a wall. "It's just... You know, it was a rough day, and the first thing I wanted to do is talk to you so I could feel better. Not my aunt or Kelsie. You. How did that happen?"

"Ye tell me, sweetheart," I said through a thick throat. "Why was your day rough?"

She sucked in another long inhale. "It's a long story. We had a surprise addition to the family dinner, and it shocked me and I didn't behave very well. The person has gone now, but I'm still shaken."

"No one likes surprises."

She gave a squawk of a laugh. "That's exactly what I said."

"Walk me through it."

"It's a big topic. And my head is pounding with a stress headache. Can you wait until we're together again to hear it all? It'll be easier not to make myself sound like a jerk."

"No way could ye make me think that."

"Oh, Ewan, even this short conversation has lifted some of the pressure off me. You made me feel better."

I wished I could hold her. In the dimly lit office, I hunkered down in my leather chair and closed my eyes. "If I was with ye, I'd do an even better job."

"Dirty." She chuckled.

"Hey! I was talking about giving ye a hug. Filthy mind." I tutted, and Hailey laughed again. "Where are ye now?" I added.

"In my old bedroom at Hollis and Elodie's place. They have this sprawling mansion, and it's gorgeous, but I wish I could go home already."

"I wish ye could come here now."

"I do, too."

We both seemed to hold our breaths for a moment.

"When ye get here, I have all kinds of plans for ye," I said slowly.

"Are we still talking about cuddling?"

"If ye want."

"And if I don't?" She shifted, rustling material.

"Are ye on your bed?" I adjusted my position in my chair, my groin tightening with need only Hailey gave me.

"Sure am. Door's locked. Talk to me, Ewan. Talk me through an orgasm and make me forget this terrible day. Soon, I'll be flying to see you and I can hardly wait. For now, I need this."

She didn't have to ask twice. In gruff tones, bowled over by the trust this lass placed in me, I dirty-talked her until she groaned my name. I followed quickly after, spilling into my fist like a teenager.

Four days. In just four days, she'd be in my arms once more.

I wouldn't want to let her go. Which meant I had a decision to make. I'd have to tell her about Lara, my ex, for one, and for two, sex was off the table until we'd worked through our situation.

This visit was going to be one hell of a challenge.

15

CHERRY ON THE CAKE

*H*ailey

My train arrived in Inverness station and, unlike last time I came to this corner of the world, I hadn't primed myself with romance novels featuring brawny Scotsmen.

I had my own waiting.

Excitement held me tight in its grip. Nerves had my stomach churning. I'd fled the US filled with emotion, but now, that sharpened to a focus. One man made everything better.

At the exit, I scanned the forecourt then spotted him.

Ewan.

I darted to meet him as he ran to me. Then I was crushed to his chest, his strong arms caging me in warmth and the best of all things. Him.

"Ah God, woman. Ye have no idea how good it is to see ye."

"Same." Emotion clogged my throat, and I buried my face in Ewan's neck, taking a deep inhale of his outdoorsy scent.

He lifted my chin to fit his mouth to mine. This kiss I'd dreamed about.

Ewan surprised me. Instead of devastating me with all I'd missed, he pressed his lips to mine in a chaste, sweet kiss. Except I felt the undercurrent of barely controlled hunger. He might be aiming for public-friendly, but there was no doubting his message.

Want.

Need.

All good with me.

He finally pulled away, his grin sheepish. "Can ye tell how much I missed ye? Will ye believe me this time?"

My own smile tugged at my mouth. "Take me home and show me."

He snapped a salute, tucked me under his arm, and grabbed my bag. In his car, Ewan kept hold of my fingers and drove us out into the frosty Scottish landscape. Low banks of snow lined the roadside, but it seemed right here— the opposite to back home.

"How was your visit?" Ewan asked. "By which I mean that I'm not scoping the competition, just interested in your trip."

I'd spent the previous afternoon in Edinburgh, checking out the smart city and touring the historic sites. Diane's offer to clients could include a country and city base. It would work perfectly with Ewan's business.

Not that I'd share that much. I'd already crossed the line with him and would play it by the book from now on.

"Good. I had fun. The manager of the place showed me around then took me to dinner. We spent hours just chatting all things tourism and the wonders of Scotland."

Ewan's fingers tightened around mine, and I glanced

over. He was glowering. My jaw dropped, then I burst out laughing.

"You okay there?" I asked.

"Aye?" He pursed his lips as if he wanted to ask more. "This manager, did he—"

"She," I corrected.

Ewan visibly brightened. "She!"

"Did you just get jealous?"

"Happy to admit I did. That's a new one for me."

We stopped at traffic lights, and Ewan switched his attention to me, pinning me down with the intensity of his dark gaze. "I've been having some pretty big thoughts since we were last together. It's left me a wee bit unsettled."

My pulse fluttered. "What kind of thoughts?"

He gave a single, amused shake of his head. "Ones that aren't going to get in the way of your work. Today, we're doing the tour. I'm officially on duty until the minute ye have the information ye want."

"And when that's done?"

Ewan's eyes gleamed. "Then, sweetheart, you're all mine."

With that promise, we drove on into the Cairngorms. Ewan pointed out landmarks as we went—places that would be on a wider guided tour option—but when we drove over the border of his land, the real draw of the McClintock business was revealed. The package Diane wanted to offer included hiking trips, where our clients would stay in Ewan's accommodation and be fully catered for with everything they'd need for several days of exploring. To that point, Ewan drove me to the trail heads and out to the beauty spots.

The first, a circle of standing stones perched on a hill, was dusted with snow and picture-perfect.

I took shots to share with Diane and the professional photographer we'd book, but also brought Ewan into one just for me.

The next site was the ruins of a castle. Even in the bitter cold, I couldn't imagine a better spot for a picnic, come summer, of course. Mountains rose around us, a winter sports resort visible on swooping slopes.

"I'll take ye skiing during your visit," Ewan promised. "Seeing as we didn't get to do it in Manhattan."

"I'd love that." I crunched across the grass to the car where I made notes on what I'd seen, and the sorts of language we'd use to sell the experience to clients.

For a couple of hours, we mapped the estate, then Ewan drove me back to the Cock Bridge Inn. In easy, heartfelt words, he talked me through the refurbishment on the cottages, and I approved the work, recognising the efforts he'd put in since his presentation.

It was fabulous. Perfect.

Tension grew between us.

Ewan's professional tone was undermined by the way his gaze stripped me bare. Likewise, I kept losing concentration and found myself simply staring at the handsome Scot.

We emerged into the low afternoon light, the inn illuminated at the other end of the track.

"Got enough?" Ewan muttered.

I was lightheaded and heady with lust. "Uh-huh. I need to write it up properly but I love all of it."

Ewan grunted and grabbed my arm. With long strides, he marched me down a lane. At the end were two sweet-looking stone houses, divided by a row of trees and with gardens around them.

"Is this you? I thought you lived in the inn."

Ewan didn't answer. Instead, he turned to me and, in a

flash, I was in his arms and laughing.

He carried me to his gate and pointed at the other house. "I've had this cottage since I was nineteen, when I was able to restore it. Briana lives there. My da's place is a short drive away, but he's gone for the week to a relative's, so we won't see him."

"How did you wrangle that?"

"A cousin of mine is a clan chief. Callum McRae is his name. I knew that Da couldn't refuse the invitation to see in the New Year in their castle, and the man was happy to oblige. He knows the struggles of running a business up here."

"Ooh, a castle."

"See? Impressive, aye? More than my ruins?"

"Nothing impresses me more than you."

At the end of the path, he opened the cottage door, carried me over the threshold like a new bride, then set me on my feet. I walked into a stone corridor, my heels sinking into a thick rug.

"Lounge. Kitchen-diner. Boot room and downstairs bathroom." Ewan flipped on lights and pointed around.

A cosy living room opened out to my right, a bright kitchen the other side. At the top of the hall, a wooden staircase ran upstairs.

"Three beds and a nice bathroom upstairs," he continued.

I lowered my eyes. "This is lovely. Want to show me your bedroom?"

"Glad ye like it. You have an hour to write up your report. Then you're mine."

I took a sharp breath, his tone turning me on even more. "What if I need longer?"

His lips twitched as if he knew this wasn't going to take

me long. "I'm going to cook dinner. Get changed, if ye want, and type fast."

I swallowed and made the mistake of looking into his eyes.

God and all the angels. Ewan stared back with pure, steadfast devotion.

I liked that far too much. That instant surge came over me again, of need and desire.

"Okay," I managed.

"Good." He kissed my forehead then moved past me to bound upstairs with my bag.

---

*A*n hour later, curled up on Ewan's comfortable sofa, I finished my write-up for Diane. She and I had already talked through Ewan's presentation and drafted a brochure. My visit today was the cherry on the cake of a great new vacation offer.

With care, I'd detailed the different options and pricing, wrote up the beautiful description that would sell the place, added my work to an email, and scheduled it to go to Diane in the morning.

Tomorrow was New Year's Eve, and I didn't want any reason to have to return sooner than January first, at least.

Laptop closed, I picked up my wine glass and leaned to peer out of the open door. Across the hall, Ewan hustled in the kitchen, making something that sent tendrils of delicious scent my way. Herbs, for certain. Thyme and sage. Mmm, rosemary, too.

As if sensing my gaze, he lifted his attention from the kitchen table. "Ye done?"

I unfurled my legs and rose, slinking my way over

to him.

A deep drink of my wine buoyed my confidence, not that it was lacking, and my thoughts shifted back to the main event. Work was over. Playtime had begun.

"All done. I'm off the clock. What's cooking?"

"Roast chicken. It's a cold night, and we need fuelling up."

"Oh yeah? What for?"

With a sweep of his forearm, Ewan cleared a space on the table, grabbed me, and perched me on the wood. Now, in private, a wave of raw, potent sexual energy rolled off him. He kissed me like I'd wanted him to all day. A hard, punishing kiss that curled my toes in my ballet flats. I wrapped my legs around his waist, putting his thick body in place between my thighs. He moved his lips on mine, and I tangled my fingers in his hair, needing him as close as I could get him.

His tongue entered my mouth, and I moaned.

He'd been right, holding back. I'd wanted to jump his bones the moment I saw him, but work had been a burden. Well, it wasn't a problem now.

"I wanted to talk," he said, breaking off to kiss my neck. "But there's twenty minutes left on the oven timer, and that's just enough time to do what I want to ye."

"Which is?"

He ran a hand under my legs and lifted me, then we were out of the kitchen and up the stairs. In his bedroom, which I'd poked around when I'd changed out of my traveling clothes, Ewan laid me on the bed and fell on top of me. We rolled, getting back into a kiss even as our hands moved to strip the other.

My t-shirt, bra, and yoga pants came off in short order. I managed to get Ewan's t-shirt off his broad frame before he was on my body, his big hands and hot mouth homing in on my breasts.

I gasped and arched into his touch, loving the way his tongue swirled my nipples into hard peaks, and how his thumb elongated them before pinching hard.

I moaned now, the afternoon of work a warm-up for what was going to be spectacular sex.

He growled appreciation then sat on his haunches. "Up the bed. Back to me. Hold the bedstead and keep your hands there."

Heart pounding, I crawled forward to do as he asked, spreading my knees wide and dressed in nothing but my tiny pink lace panties. I peered over my shoulder to see Ewan strip his jeans and boxers then fist his huge erection.

God!

A drawer provided a condom, then Ewan knelt behind me. He kissed my neck, his hot breath stirring a lock of my hair, and both of his hands took my waist. His hard body pressed to mine, his dick at my ass, and he slid a hand down to cup me between the legs.

"Good lass," he said, gruff. "Always so wet for me."

My breathing shuddered, and I dropped my head back so he could kiss me as he played. With two fingers, he drove circles into my clit, at the same time, manoeuvring so his rigid dick glided between my legs.

I rode the edge of him, working him back and forth over my entrance, though not taking him inside.

We both groaned at the sensation.

His hardness against my soft, wet centre.

Then, just as the first tendrils of an orgasm spread inside me, Ewan retreated and slammed home. In one hard hit, he filled me, a raw chuckle the reply to my gasp. Without pause, he fucked me, still moving his hand on my clit.

It was too much and not enough. Pleasure bloomed where he hit me inside, over and over, then amplified the orgasm he'd already started. A wave crashed over me, and I dropped forward, clutching the wooden rail of the bed. Around his thrusting dick, I tightened and released in pulses that blew my mind.

Ewan banded an arm around my chest and pulled me upright. He placed a hand on the wall ahead of us and fucked me like a machine.

Drive after drive into my willing flesh.

Then he, too, was coming. "Hailey," he shouted.

Inside me, he swelled and throbbed, his hands clamping me to him. We tumbled to the bed.

What a reunion. Fast, hot, and highly satisfactory.

Downstairs, a beeping sound drifted up.

"Food's done," Ewan mumbled.

I laughed and rolled so I could hug him. "Good. You've given me an appetite."

"For food or for me?" He kissed my forehead, his breathing coming in hard pulls.

"Both."

"Good," he said, then his mouth took mine, and we kissed until the timer stopped and Ewan jumped from the bed, grinning as he ran downstairs naked to save our meal.

After a minute, I followed, admiring his clean and tidy house as I passed the rooms. With polished wood, stone, filled bookshelves, and family pictures, it was the opposite of my minimalist apartment.

A family home, where it was all too easy to picture children darting out of bedrooms and running down the stairs to find their dad.

If I thought myself in trouble with Ewan before, I was in real hot water now.

16

THREE! TWO! ONE!

*E**wan*

The inn glowed with warm light, and a cheer went up as Hailey and I entered. Yesterday, after dinner, I'd brought her here for a drink and to reacquaint her with Briana plus introduce her to other relatives.

Tonight was New Year's Eve. Hogmanay, as we called it here.

There was whisky to be drunk, a live band warming up, torches to be taken out to the courtyard and burned after midnight, and the place was thick with bodies, everyone wanting a hug and to greet my new girlfriend.

Not that we'd agreed to the term yet.

Before Hailey's arrival, I'd decided we couldn't sleep together until we'd had a how-the-hell-can-we-work conversation. That plan had gone out the window after just one kiss. She'd slept in my bed and we'd spent much of today in there, too.

I'd shelved the heavy thoughts and just let myself enjoy Hailey, and her me, but a new year started in a few hours. I wanted to go into it with Hailey being mine.

For a couple of hours, we drank and danced. Briana took Hailey to one side, and the two giggled together over whatever secrets my cousin was spilling.

I liked that all the more, too.

Hailey's friend was moving to Scotland. She'd make another friend in Briana. Asking her to give up her city life was a huge deal, but maybe, just maybe, there was enough here to make her want to stay.

Unlike Lara.

Aye, this conversation needed to happen now. My mind was fucking me over with less-than-happy thoughts.

I swallowed the last of my beer and waved at Hailey, gesturing for her to follow me. She rose from the crowded corner and weaved her way to my side, then I led her out of the busy bar and to my office.

"Sneaky." She hopped onto my desk, her cheeks red with the good time she was having.

"I need to talk to ye." I switched on the lamp and sat in my leather chair, facing her.

"Are you breaking up with me?" she asked on a breath. "Right now? Right before midnight?"

"Naw, woman. The opposite. I want to talk about..." I gestured between us.

Her mouth formed a perfect O.

"I wanted to do this earlier today, but we got sidetracked. I want to know everything there is to know about ye. I want ye to tell me what upset ye on Christmas Day. I might have a few things to share myself. A sad story for one."

Hailey took a deep breath. "Is this about Lara? Two or three people have told me today that it's great to see you over her and moving on. That's your ex-girlfriend, right?"

"Aye, and more. I was engaged to her."

"Holy shit. Really?"

"Lara and I were together in school then on and off as adults. Her parents adored me, and Da wasn't too horrible to her. We made sense, so I proposed because it was expected of me. Finally, last year, she dumped my arse and moved away."

Hailey winced. "I'm sorry."

"Thank ye. I'm not."

"No? Sounds like she was the love of your life."

"I thought so at one point, but I was wrong." I stood and paced to the other side of the office then back again. "I like ye, Hailey. More than I've ever liked anyone, though we're right at the beginning. Give me a few days, and I'll be a goner."

"God," she almost whispered. "How can you know that?"

The question didn't really need an answer, because I knew she felt it, too, the fierce draw. The delight at being together.

"I know because it's impossible to ignore. So here's the problem. Lara broke my heart by leaving me. I'm glad she did because I would've been settling for familiar happiness over big love, but I can't go through that again. I don't want to hurt ye either, so if ye don't want me in the same way, I need to know now so I don't let myself fall in love with ye."

Shock registered in her expression.

Her mouth opened, but no words came out. Then she tried again. "I live in New York."

"Aye. That's an issue."

"All my friends and family are in the States. My job."

I dug my fingers into my hair and groaned. "I know. Those are important to ye."

Hailey's words flowed as if she couldn't stop them. "They are, but it's complicated, too. My father just got out of jail and blindsided me at Christmas dinner. He rang on the doorbell, and Hollis sent me to answer, meaning for it to be a wonderful surprise."

She walked me through the scene of coming face to face with her miserable, negligent father, and my heart ached.

"All through my childhood, he was a terrible dad. He'd ignore me and pass me off to strangers when he had stuff to do. We moved from crappy apartment to sofa surfing over and over, and then he went to jail and I finally got a reprieve. Hollis and Elodie gave me stability and love."

My stomach sank because I could see where this was going. "I'm sorry ye were hurt."

"I don't blame them for going along with Dad's idea. Hollis was so caught up in hope for his brother's rehabilitation that he obviously thought I'd feel the same. But I don't, and it's petty and horrible of me."

"You're not horrible."

"I am! I don't want my father in my life any more than he already was. I'd visit him in prison every few months as a kid, and he would feign interest in me but the whole time talk to my uncle or aunt, whichever was with me, about how tough it was for him not to have any money. That hurt, and I can't forgive him, even if I try to forget." She lifted her water-filled eyes to mine. "I need to do well in my job because I can't have anyone think I'm like him. Not ever."

"Sweetheart, they won't. No one who ever met ye could doubt how incredible ye are."

She sniffed. "I left all of that behind. I have to go back and fix it."

"What does fixing it entail?"

"I don't know."

My heart sank, because Hailey wasn't saying what I wanted to hear. The unreasonable demand that shouted loud in my head to get her to stay.

She wasn't even saying she wanted to try, only that fixing her life back home was her priority.

She swiped at a tear. "I know what you want me to say but I don't know... All I'm sure about is that I don't want to hurt you."

A thud shook the door.

"Not now," I yelled.

"Sorry, Ewan, but you need to come out," Briana called through the wood.

I swung the door open. "What is it?"

"Your da's here. Blathering about first footing, though he's early."

Oh fuck, no. "Shite. He was meant to be away."

Hailey appeared at my side. "Why is this a problem? Is it to do with me?"

Briana gave me a meaningful look, and I sighed, knowing my cousin was judging me for not telling Hailey this already.

"He's agreed to the changes we're making to the place, don't worry about that. I need to go and manage him. Give me a minute."

I strode to the bar, following the bellow of Da's voice over the music.

"For Auld Lang Syne," he roared against a rock and roll track.

"Da!" I grabbed his attention.

Through bleary, red eyes, he peered at me from where he stood in the centre of my family group. "There ye are, ye wee fucker. Thought you'd send me away then take your old man's spot tonight, aye?"

In his hand, he held a lump of coal and a silver coin, a bottle of whisky, and a scorched bun in the other—all the items needed for the first person over the threshold after midnight.

I'd intended to be the one carrying out this tradition as Da wasn't meant to be here.

The whisky was mostly empty. Ah grand, he was drunk.

He waggled the bottle. "Cannae get rid of me that easily."

"I'm not trying to," I said through gritted teeth, though that wasn't exactly true. I'd needed Da away so the final push could be done to finish the renovations and win the contract.

It would've worked. As a done deal, with the cash under his nose, he would've been a happy man. After a while, anyway.

Da's gaze settled on something over my shoulder, and darkened. "Ye," he bit out. "What is she doing here? I thought I told ye I wouldnae do business with those under-handed, jumped-up—"

"Da!" I knew without looking that Hailey was behind me.

"Ten! Nine! Eight," people around us called, counting down the new year.

"No. We are naw doing business with that company. I told ye I won't work with those Americans!"

"Shut your mouth," I snapped. Years of resentment flowed out through my muscles and crested in pure frustration.

I closed the distance to Da and took his arm, guiding him back outside the inn.

In the icy courtyard, I glared at him. "Ye have to stop. Ye keep pushing this business into the ground, but guess what? I won't allow it. We have families to support. Mouths to feed."

"Six! Five!" the call continued from inside.

"Ewan?" Hailey touched my shoulder.

Da homed in on the touch, his beady eyes gleaming. "I knew it. I could tell! Ye must think I was born yesterday. You're in bed with her."

"Three! Two! One!"

Cheers erupted from the inn, and I spun around to Hailey.

Eyes wide, she stared up at me.

Right now, I should be kissing her—a new tradition I wanted to put in place, to kiss her every year and bring us luck for the months to come, where we'd be a couple and in love—but she wasn't mine. Not in the way I wanted.

Da's angry shout had me spinning back.

A few staggered meters away, he'd clamped a phone to his ear. "Diane Kudrow? Ye listen here. If ye think ye can send a floozie to sleep with my son to win my business—"

"No!" I stormed to him and snatched for the phone.

Da evaded me. "I willnae have it! Call off your wee prostitute and keep your nose out of my business."

I grabbed again, this time connecting with the phone, and I killed the call.

Da grinned, the smug old drunk, but Hailey had clasped her hands to her mouth.

"Did your dad just tell Diane that I'm sleeping with you?"

"Shite." I put my hands out to her, palms down as if I could placate her.

"That's my career gone," she uttered. "And your business hopes. All in one phone call."

Briana appeared at the door. "Old Mac. How could ye?"

Da wobbled on his feet, and my cousin grabbed his arm then gestured to me. "Get in there to do the first footing before there's a riot, then get him home. I'll take care of Hailey."

"No. Hailey—"

But my lass dropped her gaze to the floor. "Go ahead. I… Fuck. I need to get away." She took off down the track, Briana skittering after her.

Leaving me to clear up Da's mess, yet again.

17

RED LIGHT FLASHED

Hailey
Gray skies received me in New York, and I exited the plane, exhausted and hurting so badly inside it was if my heart had been torn in two.

After last night's horrible showdown with Ewan's dad, I'd gone to Briana's cottage and stayed there. Ewan had come to find me, but I'd told him I needed to sleep then get on the first plane home.

He'd let me go, and now, I was here and he was there.

I'd hated every minute of flying away. Except I had to.

Even if my career was over, I could save Ewan's business.

In fact, if Diane hadn't yet checked in with the company voicemail, I might even be able to save both.

My cab flew through the city, and I jumped out at Park Avenue to grab my office keys. Twenty minutes later, I was opening the door to Kudrow International Travel.

Diane raised her head from the reception desk, her hand on the phone.

Its red light flashed. A message waiting.

My stomach tightened, and every cell of my body went cold.

"Hailey? What are you doing here? I figured you'd be enjoying the delights of Scotland for a couple more days."

I couldn't detect her tone so I forced a rigid smile. "I just got back and have a few things to do."

"Diligent as ever. I had to pick up my laptop, then I'm going home. I'm going to make a coffee for the road. Want one?"

"Sure thing," I squeaked.

Diane breezed to her small office at the back of the shop, and I hurried to the flashing phone. I pressed the answerphone button, and a loud voice blared.

"Message one. Received January First—"

"Eep!" I picked up the handset, stopping the loudspeaker.

In my ear, Old Mac's rant played out.

My chest tightened, and I held in a sob then selected Delete to forever rid the world of that awful experience.

"Was that anyone important?" Diane called.

"Nope," I trilled back, stifling tears.

I slumped in the chair. My mad dash home had taken my energy and destroyed it. All my fears for Ewan's business lifted, but I couldn't bring myself to be happy. Right now, I needed to crawl back to my empty apartment and hide in my bed.

Diane appeared at my shoulder, her travel mug in hand and a cup for me. I took the coffee on autopilot.

"You're overdoing it," my boss observed. "It's a brand-new year. Go on home, and I'll see you in the morning."

"You're right." I sat up. "Did you get a chance to read my reports from Scotland?"

"Hmm? Oh yes. Excellent work. I've already made the offer to the Castletons."

That was the Edinburgh people. "What about the McClintocks?"

Diane waved her mug and swung open the door. "Ah, no. We won't be working with them. I've decided we need to find a larger provider so we're back to square one. Actually, you might as well let them know, since you're here. I'm so grateful to have you. This hard work will stand you in very good stead for next month's assessment. See you tomorrow."

She left, and I stared after her.

Ewan had lost the contract.

My gut crunched, and I sobbed, tears flowing now. After everything, I'd lost him and he'd lost all he'd worked for. What a terrible, awful outcome.

As I sat there crying, realization dawned slowly in my tired mind. Diane had stated that I was in good form for my assessment, the one that turned this temporary job into a permanent one.

I didn't care.

I took a shuddering breath, wondering at my turn around in attitude. This job had been everything for me. I didn't need it anymore.

I'd left my heart in Scotland.

In a haze of astonishment, I opened the nearest laptop and logged on to my email. Then I wrote a note to Diane. Friendly, so not to burn bridges, but very much deciding my future with Kudrow International Travel.

A quick stop off at the penthouse saw my bags packed. In no time, I had cleared my room, which told me everything about how far I'd put down roots in this beautiful minimalist home. Every piece of furniture belonged to Hollis and Elodie, happily borrowed by me but easy to walk away from. Then I exited the city almost as quickly as I'd arrived into it. In a couple of hours, I was arriving at my aunt and uncle's house in Connecticut.

"Hailey! What are you doing here?" On the front doorstep, Elodie swept me into a sideways hug, her bump between us.

I wanted to sag against her. "Making a mistake. I should be on the next plane to Scotland but I needed to come here first. I'm so sorry about my attitude on Christmas Day."

Elodie pursed her lips and guided me inside. "Now now, none of that. Hollis was so annoyed at himself for not seeing the bigger picture. All your dad did was talk about how everyone else could help him. We're both sorry to have ruined your day."

My uncle emerged from the den and came straight to me with his arms wide. "I heard all of that. I owe you an apology and an explanation. Come on, there's something I've been meaning to tell you."

In their lovely living room, Hollis sat me down and fixed me with a look. "I made a mistake in your father. All our lives, I've believed that Stephen could be a good man, with the right help. But some people can't be saved. I've accepted that now, and it's helped me see him for what he is."

"A selfish loser," I suggested.

Hollis sighed and pushed back his blond hair, the same shade as mine. "Indeed. I'm pretty certain he stole from me, too. Remember the money I set aside for the staff at Christmas? All the envelopes were gone."

I slammed my palm to my forehead. In my upset, I'd forgotten all about that. "God! No, that was me. I hid them in your desk when he arrived. I'm so sorry."

My uncle blinked but gave a laugh. "You had better foresight that me. Did you think he'd take them?"

"Perhaps. It was kinder not to test him."

"Thank you for that." Hollis exchanged a look with his wife then leaned in. "Did I ever tell you that before you were born, he used your mom's pregnancy to extort money out of our mother?"

"No!"

"Sad but true."

I shook my head in regret. "Do you think he got mom pregnant just to make money?"

Hollis and Elodie winced.

"It's a possibility," my uncle conceded. "But you were wanted. We wanted you."

I was glad for it. And lucky.

I told them so, and Elodie smiled. "Then tell us, what's in Scotland?"

With rising excitement, I told them the new but thrilling plan I'd concocted on the journey here. And about Ewan. All about my wonderful Scot.

When I finished, Elodie dabbed her eyes, unashamed of her emotions. "One question: Do you want to see your father again before you do this thing?"

"Honestly, I couldn't care less about seeing him. He's just a sperm donor. You two have been the only parents I've ever wanted, and I came here first because of that. I need you to know that I love you."

"Ah honey, we love you, too." Hollis hugged me again. "Does that mean we're allowed to come visit soon?"

I leaned in. "I'd love that. Soon and often. I have a business proposal first, if you'll hear it."

"Anything for you."

Part two of my newly envisioned but long-dreamed-about plan was agreed, and by the time I left, I had my energy back and I was gunning for the next chapter of my life.

Part one. To get my man.

Outside the front door, my father waited.

"Hailey!" he blinked at me, his thatch of pale hair a mess. "Didn't know you were going to be here."

I sighed and tried not to see him for everything he wasn't. "Hi, Dad. I came by to say farewell to Hollis and Elodie."

He raised his chin but gazed past me. "They in?"

I summoned my patience. "I'm moving to Scotland."

"Yeah, but who's going to fix my car? I said to Hollis that a secondhand one was a waste of his money. I only pushed the speed to check the engine was sound, and next thing I know, it's breaking down in the middle of the highway."

My father. Gifted a car, an apartment, and a family, but still wanting more.

I let the grief for my parent wash over me and smiled. "Maybe you should thank Hollis and go and try to fix it yourself?"

Then I left. This time, for good.

18

HOW…?

E wan

Across the Cock Bridge Inn's bar, Briana watched me. "It'll be okay, ye ken."

"How do ye know that? We lost the contract." I stared into my glass of water, wishing I could hit the whisky instead.

But it was nine AM, and I had a new business model to develop. Yesterday, January second, an email landed in my account. A gentle letdown from Diane Kudrow. She loved our proposal but ultimately, we were too small for her.

Which left me with a huge debt of investment and no obvious source of spring and summer bookings.

"Ye never know. Things might brighten up soon." Briana's voice held a tease.

I couldn't see how.

I'd lost everything. My lass, my business, and possibly my home which I could sell to fix this mess. It was better than laying off staff, yet still, my heart hurt.

The inn door creaked open. "We're naw serving breakfast today," I griped without looking up. "Drinks start at eleven. Sorry."

"What if I don't want either? What if I'm here for something else entirely?"

I swung up my gaze to find Hailey in the entrance, an enormous suitcase behind her.

Briana chuckled and exited the bar.

Leaving us alone.

My pulse raced, and I staggered up from my stool. "You're here. God, woman. How...?"

Hailey took a step toward me. "I'm here because of one thing. You."

"Ye are?" I could only stare.

"Diane already told you about the proposal failing, didn't she? She'd asked me to do it then went ahead herself. I'm sorry I couldn't call before then but I've been running around like crazy, getting myself ready to come here."

"I don't understand."

Hailey dragged her case over the threshold and closed the sunny winter's day out, then edged closer, her gaze taking in my face.

I probably looked terrible. I'd barely slept since she left.

"I missed you," she uttered.

My heart skipped a beat.

"I missed you and I care so much about you. All I want is to be with you. I knew it last week but I was scared."

"Ye still want me?"

Hailey's lips crinkled as if she was fighting emotion. "I do. You said to me that if you let yourself, you could fall for me. Is that still possible? Can you try?" She sniffed, and a fast tear ran down her cheek. Another step brought her closer still. "Promise I didn't break us completely."

My shackles fell away, and I stood, pulling her into my

arms. This moment was my test. I'd fallen hard for her, so quickly it was unreal. But if she'd truly come for me then that meant everything. "Sweetheart, tell me you're here to stay."

"Yes!" Hailey burst into tears and clung to me.

"Then you're mine. I'm yours. We're official."

I held her tight then brought her mouth to mine.

For a long while, reunited, we kissed and made up.

The door opened again, and two newcomers walked in, amusement on their faces at our clinch.

Hailey glanced up and smiled. "Ewan, let me introduce Hollis and Elodie, my uncle and aunt. Guys, this is my Ewan."

Her Ewan.

I loved the sound of that.

Hailey rubbed her hands together. "Now it's time for business."

For the next hour, with Briana at my side, Hailey and her family outlined a proposal they'd developed, mostly on the flight over, from what I could gather, to set Hailey up as a locally based travel agent, specialising in holidays between the US and Scotland. She'd be the spokeswoman for multiple small, independent businesses like mine, and a trusted American face of the company, which meant occasional trips back to the States where she'd see her family. But ninety-five percent of her time would be spent in Scotland. With me.

The first place on her books? The Cock Bridge Inn.

Briana punched my shoulder, and I hugged my lass.

The future looked bonnie after all.

EPILOGUE

*H*ailey – *February*
The cool breeze played with my hair, and I climbed from my car, gesturing to Kelsie and her husband at the beautiful view. Ahead, the castle ruins spread across the hillside, a few hikers braving the chilly day.

"I'll show you around," I said to my best friend.

She'd arrived last week, and we'd fallen straight back into our easy friendship, seeing each other a lot despite the rapid rate I'd set up my and Ewan's new business.

For the past month, I'd worked almost every hour I could. Ewan had been right by my side. Except for at night.

Both of us knew we needed to pace ourselves to make a solid foundation for our relationship. When I'd arrived at the inn in January, all I'd wanted was to proclaim my love to everyone who'd listen.

But it was way too soon.

In fact, I'd taken a room at the inn and slept there. Mostly. Ewan and I needed grounding and had agreed to take it slow. Now, with our website up and running and bookings already starting, we were winning.

"No need to show us around." Kelsie, who'd organized this day out, gave me a meaningful look then pointed in the other direction.

Ewan crossed the open plateau. I hadn't seen him last night or this morning. That had been way too long.

"Go to him," my friend urged. "We'll find our own way around."

She didn't need to tell me twice. I hastened over, my happiness complete.

As I got closer, I spied the picnic blanket in a quiet, hidden spot. Then I ogled the man himself, as, despite the low temperature, Ewan had donned a kilt. *Whoa, mama.*

He growled his happiness and snatched me into his arms. But before we could get reacquainted in the way I really wanted, with a lovely, long kiss, Ewan put me down and backed up a step.

And sank to one knee.

Shock had me snapping my hand to my mouth. We hadn't even said that we loved each other, and he was about to...

In a fluid move, Ewan produced a gold key from his pocket and held it out. "Hailey LaCroix, you're my one and only, and I've fallen so hard in love with ye that ye have me reeling. These past few weeks have been the best of my life and I want, no, I beg ye to accept this key. Move in with me, aye?"

I pressed my hands to my mouth then laughed joyously.

"God, yes! I love you, too!"

Ewan leapt up and grabbed me.

Our kiss would make anyone blush.

Laughter across the way told me Kelsie agreed.

"By the way," he continued conversationally, "the next time I do this, it'll be a ring I'm holding up and my name offered for ye to accept. Then we'll be planning far more than just ye moving in."

My heart panged because heck yes, I loved that idea. Marrying the Scot? Bring it on. I kissed him and played down my excitement. "So sure I'll say yes."

Of course I would, because this man, and our hopefully successful grass-roots business, was everything. Even his apologetic father approved.

I loved Ewan McClintock, and my dreams of getting my own cocky kilted Scot had finally come true.

The End.

R ead more in the Cocky Hero Club series here: http://www.cockyheroclub.com/

Add yourself to the mailing list here:

http://www.cockyheroclub.com/join-our-mailing-list.html

--

Like Jolie's delicious and brawny Scotsmen? There are two series full of them - Marry the Scot and Wild Scots.

Keep reading to devour chapter one of Storm the Castle (Marry the Scot, #1) but first, add yourself to Jolie's insider list: https://www.jolievines.com/newsletter

ALSO BY JOLIE VINES

Marry the Scot series

1) Storm the Castle

2) Love Most, Say Least

3) Hero

4) Picture This

5) Oh Baby

Wild Scots series

1) Hard Nox

2) Perfect Storm

3) Lion Heart

4) Fallen Snow

5) Stubborn Spark

Wild Mountain Scots series

1) Obsessed

Standalones

Race You: An Office-Based Enemies-to-Lovers Romance

Fight For Us: a Second-Chance Military Romantic Suspense

Visit and follow my Amazon page for all new releases amazon.com/author/jolievines

Add yourself to my insider list to make sure you don't miss my publishing news https://www.jolievines.com/newsletter

STORM THE CASTLE (A MARRY THE SCOT NOVEL) BY JOLIE VINES

CHAPTER ONE - A WALL OF MAN

Mathilda

As a little girl, I'd dreamt of hearing the words 'Marry me'. Soft music playing in the background and a ring offered from my lover's eager hands. This, of course, was before my closest example of marriage became a warning rather than an inspiration.

My childish, rose-tinted vision had never involved me standing in the corner of a glittering conference, freaking out over the proposal I'd just received.

Dominic Hanswick, my father's business partner, had watched Dad leave then taken me to one side. He'd been polite and concise as he'd laid out his terms. "Marry me, Mathilda. Save my reputation. Save your sister in the process. Think about it. I'm sure you'll find it a reasonable idea." He'd offered it so easily then he'd smiled and moved away through the tables, murmuring pleasantries to colleagues.

A business deal, he'd called it.

Who said things like that?

My head already ached like I'd been in a hit-and-run,

the dreadful lunch I'd had at my parents' home still forefront in my mind. Scarlet's behaviour was the only reason I wasn't laughing this off.

Shocked, I'd barely asked Dominic any questions, but now dozens came to mind. God, he wouldn't expect me to sleep with him, would he?

I needed answers, and standing around in my flat sandals wasn't getting me anywhere. My job for the evening was done—I was only at the event as a favour to Dad, meaning I could leave and return to my hotel, but this had thrown me for a loop. With a calming breath, I left the safety of my alcove and crossed the hall.

"Mr Hanswick?" I tapped the shoulder of his smart suit, and the man turned. My would-be fiancé was a businessman, a senior partner with Storm Enterprises, the conglomerate my father ran. He was smart, had the stout figure of a man used to finer things, and at forty-two, seventeen years my senior.

Overall, Dominic was not what I had in mind when I'd envisaged my groom.

"If you have a moment, I need to ask a quick question." A vast understatement. I backed away from the group, smiling at people important to my dad. The model of a dutiful daughter.

Dominic excused himself and followed. His brow crinkled. "You have my business card. Set up a meeting, and we can talk through the finer details."

Right. And yet, "You said you wanted a marriage of convenience. In name only."

He glanced around, presumably to make sure we were out of earshot. "Naturally."

"What happens if I want to date someone?" Why was that so important? I hadn't dated anyone in months.

He sighed. "The point of selecting you, Mathilda, is that you're young, single, and practical. My home is big enough for us to live separate lives: you with your sister on one side, me on the other. This arrangement works for all involved. As for other...needs you might have, sleep with whomever you choose, but I'd recommend you stick to one-night stands. At least until we near the end of the five years. And for Heaven's sake, be discreet. I've had enough scandal to last a lifetime, and a cheating wife would set me back to square one."

"I see." I nodded along like this was anything other than insane. I knew Dominic had been the subject of press attention. He'd had an affair with a high-profile, married politician, and the newspapers had made a meal over it. Dad had ranted about the effect it had on Storm Enterprise's shareholders, so I knew Dominic was losing money fast.

Getting married would fix his reputation and save his bank balance.

None of this was my problem.

Scarlet's emotional health, on the other hand, was. Her chance at having a good future.

As if sensing my reticence, the man leaned in. Even though I was in my flats, my six-foot height meant I was looking down on him. "Your sister is off the rails. You can help her. Why wouldn't you do that? Your father will let you take her in if you're married, am I correct?"

How on Earth did he know that? I gave a slow nod. From behind me came the clamour of raised voices. Dominic's attention shifted to the source of the commotion, and his eyes widened as if in recognition. He gave me a short bow. "I have to leave. Call my assistant to set up that meeting, and we can finalise the arrangements. Just don't take a time over it. It serves us both to arrange this as soon as possible."

Then he was gone.

Rotating, I spied a vacant table in a dark corner. On the way, I grabbed a glass of water from a waiter then found a chair and laid my head back. My sister, Scarlet, nearly arrested again last week, worried me to death, and clearly Dominic knew enough about the situation to determine which buttons to push. It was the solitary reason I'd have to say yes, saving her skin and, separately, his, and why I hadn't yet laughed him out of town.

Not that I would do anything quite so unladylike.

A surge of frustration filled me from even entertaining the idea. I didn't want Dominic. He'd called me practical, and I was, but what about chemistry and heat and passion? I wanted more than the lacklustre relationships I'd so far suffered in my twenty-five years on the planet. Beth, my best friend, made a robot-Mathilda voice when I was being ultra-efficient, but inside I was like everyone else: desiring that overwhelming romance. The breathless appetite-quenching satisfaction that came from sex with someone I loved.

The love stories I devoured couldn't all be wrong.

If I took the marriage deal, on whatever terms, I wouldn't have the chance to find out. Then again, who's to say I'd ever find this relationship utopia. My last boyfriend had cheated, after all. Maybe a sham marriage and one-night stands could work. Passion based on the purely phys-ical was better than nothing.

At the entranceway, a distance across the open hall, two men emerged through the crush. Both tall, the men carried a watchful air as the event's patrons left a moat around them, and my interested gaze skipped over each as they shook off the security staff.

The dark-haired younger man had the kind of looks you could stare at for an hour and praise God for pretty people.

But it was the man beside him who caught my attention. And held it. Because *holy hell.*

Not only because of his size—he was one of the tallest men I'd ever seen—but for the way people orbited around him, and how he held his powerful, large body with ease as he reached out a long arm to take a glass of what appeared to be water. He gave the waiter a polite nod, and I warmed inside.

Lifting my drink, I tried not to stare. *"Good luck with that."* I imagined my friend's stage-whisper. If only Beth could be here to ogle alongside me. She'd nab a cocktail, rest her chin on her hands, and goggle freely.

The room lights flickered over the doorway, as if showing off for the big man, and a lick of interest curled in my belly.

Power impressed me. I couldn't help the fact.

Then, like I'd switched on a neon light that said "Look over here, big guy!" the man's gaze swept over the busy space and locked onto mine. I started, but he didn't move on as would be proper. Instead, he angled his head and ran an attentive glance over me. A fair eyebrow raised, appreciation lightening his serious expression.

The babbling noise of the room ramped up, and I dragged in a breath. Heat snaked under my high-necked dress, maybe from the intensity or maybe from the humidity, and I tore my gaze away, fidgeting on the chair. *Wow.*

If I was to ever try a one-night stand, he'd be top of my list.

Then my head panged again, and I winced. My cue to leave. From my bag, I extracted my phone to book an Uber, and on the screen, a message already waited. Beth.

Testing testing, are you still alive? Did your dad make you do a speech?

I tapped out a reply.

Luckily, no. But he did tell a bunch of his colleagues that I'd be working for him soon. I should've just come home after lunch.

I'd journeyed to London this morning to see my family, and I could've been on the first train home to the house I shared with Beth. Instead, I'd gritted my teeth through an awful lunch, politely kissed my mother goodbye, booked into a hotel, then attended Dad's product launch. They thought I was getting the late train, though I hated travelling at night, otherwise I'd be forced to stay at my family's home. The mere thought had me shuddering.

Beth shot back an answer as Uber gave me a twelve-minute wait time.

Ugh, I'm sorry, honey. Want me to come get you tonight?

It was a generous offer, and a long drive, but I was too rattled by Dominic's offer and by no means ready to talk about it. Beth would expect me to be miserable as each visit to see my family took me a week to get over. But this... I needed to sleep on it.

Readying to leave, I let my gaze seek out the big man one last time. From first appearance, he wasn't the type of guy I'd usually find interesting. Rougher, less refined than a standard city-dweller. At a black-tie event, he was wearing jeans, so I guessed he was in the wrong room at the conference centre. He was a tourist, maybe. Though the way he and his friend had entered the place felt more purposeful than happy holidaymakers.

A mountain man, I mused, sliding my phone into its pocket in my bag. Used to harder living and working with his hands. Maybe he had a shack somewhere he emerged from each morning to cut wood and fetch water from a stream. He'd go swimming in a river some days.

Naked, obviously.

I grinned at my own fantasy, the levity of it the most exciting part of my evening. But my search of the event space was fruitless. The shy-looking model-type stood with his back to the wall. The interesting one had vanished.

More disappointed than I reasonably should be, I took a final sip from my water then eased myself up from the table. But as I stood, the strap of my sandal snapped, and I stumbled. My purse swung in a wide arc, knocking straight into my glass.

Down the glass fell, cracking on the seat. It shattered and rained razor-edged pieces over my feet. "Shit!" I squawked. And there was me, proud of how little I swore.

I danced away, but in the process, wedged my ankle against the chair leg, trapping a piece of glass. It stung. With a wince, I fell back onto the seat and clutched at my foot, losing my shoe. A sliver of glass stuck out from my skin. I touched the edge and nearly fainted.

Blood welled, and my head swam.

"What's happened here?" a deep voice sounded beside me.

I peeked up. And up.

It was the man. A *wall* of man, looking down at me. Sweet Jesus, he had to be close to seven feet tall. The top of my head wouldn't even reach his chin.

I opened my mouth and managed, "Be careful, there's glass. My drink fell."

Then, with the worst timing, a flood of emotion came over me. My evening had turned absurd. My tiny, stinging injury was nothing compared to the impossible offer my father's colleague had made me. Worse, I couldn't think of another way to help my sister than to accept him.

Marry someone I didn't care for.

Add to that the embarrassment of being a klutz in front

of the most impressive man I'd ever seen, my horrible headache, and nausea from my lack of food, I wanted to curl up in a ball.

That was it. My head reeled double-time, my foot panged, and my brain checked out.

Like in an old-style romance novel, I swooned, and everything went black.

ead on...

ABOUT THE AUTHOR

JOLIE VINES is a romance novelist who lives in the South West of England with her husband and son.

From an early age, Jolie lived in a fantasy world and is never happier than when plot dreaming. Jolie loves her heroes to be one-woman guys. Whether they are a huge Highlander, a touch starved earl, or a brooding pilot, they will adore their loved one until the end of time.

Her favourite pastime is wrecking emotions then making up for it by giving her characters deep and meaningful happy ever afters.

Want to contact Jolie? She loves hearing from her readers. Find her on Instagram and join her Fall Hard Facebook group.